D1743854

A Challenge for
MICHAEL

A Challenge for MICHAEL

TRICIA BARISONZI-JOHNSON

Copyright © 2018 Tricia Barisonzi-Johnson.

All rights reserved. No part of this book may be used or reproduced by
any means, graphic, electronic, or mechanical, including photocopying,
recording, taping or by any information storage retrieval system
without the written permission of the author except in the case
of brief quotations embodied in critical articles and reviews.

Archway Publishing books may be ordered
through booksellers or by contacting:

Archway Publishing
1663 Liberty Drive
Bloomington, IN 47403
www.archwaypublishing.com
1 (888) 242-5904

Because of the dynamic nature of the Internet, any web addresses or
links contained in this book may have changed since publication and
may no longer be valid. The views expressed in this work are solely those
of the author and do not necessarily reflect the views of the publisher,
and the publisher hereby disclaims any responsibility for them.

Any people depicted in stock imagery provided by Getty Images are
models, and such images are being used for illustrative purposes only.
Certain stock imagery © Getty Images.

ISBN: 978-1-4808-6181-7 (sc)
ISBN: 978-1-4808-6182-4 (hc)
ISBN: 978-1-4808-6183-1 (e)

Library of Congress Control Number: 2018946710

Print information available on the last page.

Archway Publishing rev. date: 5/31/2018

I dedicate this book to my two loving sisters,

Denise Barisonzi and *Diane Barisonzi.*

INTRODUCTION

*L*ove—what a wondrous word! It can take the saddest, loneliest people and make them feel like they're soaring over the ocean.

A Challenge for Michael is about two people who meet, fall in love, and then are separated. With a twist of fate, they are brought back together again.

This book is propelled by true love. Every kiss, every embrace touches the reader, not to mention their loving, caring way of consummating their love.

To find one's soul mate is almost impossible to achieve, but these two characters find a way to get through turmoil and still prevail. A weaker person never would make it, but Michael has an inner strength and uses it in an honest way to remember what his past was like.

Every page is filled with love, even when the couple are going through the most difficult time of their marriage. Readers will become mesmerized by the deep love of the characters and perhaps apply it to their own lives to learn how to make a better life for themselves.

A Challenge for Michael is a book that the reader will want to experience more than once. It will leave you with a sense of peace in your life and perhaps lead you to your true love.

Tricia Barisonzi-Johnson

CHAPTER 1

ntoinette Lavini pushed back her seat as the captain announced they would be landing. In a few hours, she'd be back in St. Paul. For a moment, she felt completely deflated and utterly confused. What in God's name was she doing? Just getting up and leaving a life where she had finally found some form of contentment. Her position with the bathing-suit firm had been really good. In the two years she had been with them, she had managed to work herself up from one of the five assistant designers to head designer. Her natural ability for color and design had really paid off, not to mention her determination to make a better life for herself.

Toni had managed to put behind her shattered life and finally get on with living. Then the letter came from Jason, and it abruptly changed her life. She had read it over and over again until she had memorized every word and the paper was limp from handling, but it still wasn't enough. She took it from her handbag and opened it again.

My Dear Toni,

Tracy and I miss you very much and, as in previous letters, I have always tried to coerce you into coming home. I know you never felt you had a reason to as long as Michael and Terri were married, but there is good news, my dear! Or I should say *excellent* news! Michael has finally come to his senses and divorced that—well, you know what I think of her!

When she read that line, she reacted the same way she had all the times before. A ray of hope sprang from her heart. Hope! What an enchanting word! She had almost forgotten the word existed.

Now, my darling Toni, how long will it take for you to pack up and be on your way? Please call and tell us when you'll be landing.

Love,

Jason and Tracy

P.S: Tracy apologizes for not writing. You know her. She's always running around doing something.

CHAPTER 2

*S*o here she was, seated in a plane, heading back home. Thoughts from the past overwhelmed her—leaving home for school in New York and leaving Michael, the hardest thing she'd ever done in her life. And dear, sweet Noel, her manager in California. She had never meant to hurt him, but she was honest about her feelings right from the start. He risked falling in love with her. It was his choice and, unfortunately, one he would have to live with now.

She remembered Noel's face when she told him she was returning to St. Paul. It was full of dismay, as though his world were ending. She knew he hoped she had forgotten Michael, and when he asked her to marry him, she reluctantly accepted, hoping she could put her past behind her, hoping that there was no hope of ever being with Michael again.

But the truth was she could never forget Michael. He was the love of her life, her reason for living. She tried very hard to start a new life, but he was always in the back of her mind. He haunted her as if they were in love yesterday, but those yesterdays were far behind her now. She had to get on with her life.

And then the letter arrived from Jason.

"I hope you know what you're doing," Noel raged, his voice filled with anger and desperation. "I've known for the longest time you still loved Michael, but I hoped you would put him aside and make room for me in your life. It's been four years, Toni. *Four years!* How can you think of returning there and just picking up where you left off? How do you know he hasn't gone back to Terri?"

"They're divorced," Toni said matter-of-factly. She couldn't be angry with Noel. She knew how hurt he was, but she also knew that she had to return to St. Paul. There was no avoiding it. Maybe it wouldn't work out, but she had to give herself the chance, even if this meant leaving behind everything she was accustomed to.

Toni suddenly felt exhausted and drifted off to sleep.

She was awakened by the stewardess announcing they would be landing. She panicked. Good God! What was she doing? How could she go through with this? She wanted to stay on the plane and return to California. That was what her common sense told her, but this had nothing to do with her common sense—only her heart.

CHAPTER 3

As Toni walked down the jetway leading to the passenger waiting area, she was filled with apprehension, but the feeling soon dissolved when she spotted her family and then Jason and Tracy. But Michael? Where was he? Everyone was around her before she knew what had happened, hugging and kissing her and telling her how happy they were that she was back. She couldn't see past the blanket of people at the airport but strained her neck to see if she could spot him. Then she saw a man walking away. She recognized his gait immediately. Her beautiful brown eyes filled with tears, but she managed to brush them away before anyone noticed. A feeling of emptiness invaded her and brought back memories of that somber day in September when she flew out of his life.

"Honey, we found you the cutest little apartment." Her mother's voice bubbled over with enthusiasm. "We know you'll like it." She unsuccessfully attempted a smile.

"When do you start your new job at Shapiro's?" her brother, Tim, asked.

"In a week," she replied automatically, occupied with her thoughts.

Toni hadn't even thought about her new position and how she managed to land it from California. Her employer, Mr. Taylor, had given her an excellent reference, and she shipped her résumé and portfolio home immediately. After seeing them, Mr. Shapiro was happy to have her on board. Her new position would be an assistant designer for a large, successful bathing-suit company in St. Paul.

Toni realized that her new job was a demotion, but she had studied swimwear extensively in college and was anxious to continue in the field. She was confident that she would prove herself quickly and a promotion would follow.

She was anxious to start at Shapiro's as soon as possible, but loads of cartons had to be unpacked. She was hoping that getting settled would keep her mind off Michael.

CHAPTER 4

All of a sudden, high school memories flooded her. When the pencil fell, Mr. Matthews was giving a lecture on the use of the participle. He had just asked Toni a question, which she had answered eagerly. She was a good student who was very ambitious and determined to achieve. She had bent down to pick up the pencil, but his hand had reached it an instant before hers. He had turned to hand it to her, and her eyes had fallen on the most handsome boy she had ever seen—and he was smiling at her! Quickly she had murmured thanks, embarrassed by the silence in the room. Feeling as if all eyes were on her, she had managed to smile at him and then focused her attention on Mr. Matthews.

Toni hadn't been able to stop staring at his back. He sat a few seats away, and it had been hard to keep her mind on the lecture. All she could remember at the time was that his eyes were as deep blue as the ocean and his hair was thick and sandy brown. It had been hard to tell how tall he was, but she had sensed he was close to six feet. She knew then she'd have a hard time getting through the next twenty minutes of class without wondering about him.

As the bell rang, the students had risen, collected their belongings, and shuffled out into the hall. Toni had started to head in the direction of her next class when she heard a voice from behind her and turned to see him standing there. A feeling of awkwardness had overcome her as she looked into his smiling face.

"Your name is Toni, isn't it?" he'd asked, his expression filled with warmth.

"*Ye-e-e-s,*" she'd stammered. She started to walk away, but he came after her.

"Hey, what's your hurry?" he'd said, laughing softly.

"I have to get to my next class."

"Do you mind if I walk with you?"

"No," she'd replied, embarrassed by her awkwardness.

"My name is Michael. I've noticed you in class, but I guess I never knew how to break the ice."

Toni had attempted to smile and stepped up her walk.

"I didn't know you were the shy type," he'd observed.

"I'm not!" she'd blurted out. "Well, yes, I guess I am when I first meet people. I really have to go. I'll be late."

"Do you think I could call you later?" he'd asked shyly.

"Sure, that'd be okay." She'd hurriedly written down her number and then rushed off.

Michael had stood there watching her as she walked away with a puzzled look on his face. He then smiled, turned, and went to class.

CHAPTER 5

When Toni got home that afternoon, she greeted her mother warmly and then went straight to her room. She loved her bedroom, which she had decorated herself. Since the age of eight, when her grandmother taught her to sew, she would save her money for fabric and use her mom's machine to create her own wardrobe. She would buy commercial patterns and then modify them into her own designs.

When her parents realized how talented she was, they encouraged her to utilize her talent by sewing for the family. She had sewn Easter outfits every year and uniforms for Tim's band, and she did her own personal sewing.

She had spent hours making accessories for her bedroom: a coverlet, dust ruffle, and pillow shams for her bed—all done in pink. She had also used the same fabric for a skirt for her dressing table. When she wasn't able to find an ideal sewing chest in stores, she had converted an old wooden cabinet into one to meet her needs. The chest was complete with thread holders on the inside doors and sewing accessories. The outside doors had inlays in which she glued deep-blue velvet to match the powder-blue paint she had used for the cabinet and the rest of the furniture in her room. The walls were done in oak paneling and the ceiling in powder blue to match the furniture.

Toni plopped down on her bed and opened her English book. She started to read her homework assignment but couldn't keep her mind on the chapter. Thoughts of Michael kept seeping into her mind. She tried to dismiss her feelings by telling herself she was being silly, but she couldn't understand why she had been so timid with him. She had never had a problem speaking to boys before. She found them to be unpretentious, which made her feel comfortable. But with Michael, it was different. She had felt very silly just standing there, not knowing what to say. She realized it was probably because he was pretty popular in school. In fact, he was very popular. He came from a nice middle-class family. Not that her family was poor, but they were more working class. She knew people at Central High School, but not that many because she only spent her mornings there and then attended St. Paul Vocational and Technical High School in the afternoons, where she was taking advanced sewing.

Michael's father was probably an accountant or a lawyer, Toni thought, and her father worked for the City of St. Paul as a custodian. Michael's siblings would assuredly go to college, whereas Toni would be the first child in her family to get a college education. College was very important to her. She wanted a chance to better herself. All she had ever wanted since she could remember was to be a designer and follow in her grandfather's footsteps. He had spent many years designing, and before he left

New York, he had worked for Elizabeth Arden as her assistant. He finally settled in St. Paul, where he opened his own tailor shop. Her father had spent hours telling her stories about the shop.

Toni felt she had a natural talent for design. She had her life all worked out for her to go to design school in New York right after high school, and then—

The ring of the phone broke her train of thought. Toni's heart skipped a beat when she heard her brother yell from upstairs, "Hey, sis, the phone!" She got up to answer it.

"Hello?" she said shyly.

"Hi, Toni." That feeling of awkwardness came over her again. What would she say to him?

"Are you there?"

"Yes, yes, I'm here," she answered hesitantly.

"This is Michael. The guy that picked up your pencil this afternoon. Remember?"

How could she forget? "Yes, I remember. Hi, how are you?"

"Okay," he replied. "Listen, I'm calling because I was wondering if you were doing anything this Friday night. There's a good movie playing at the drive-in, and I thought you might like to go."

"Well, yes," Toni said cheerfully. "That's okay."

"We could get a bite to eat before, too. How about my picking you up at six thirty?"

"Okay," Toni agreed.

When Toni hung up the phone, she thought to herself that there was no reason why she shouldn't date. A date certainly wouldn't interfere with her plans. After all, she wasn't leaving for New York until next September. She might as well enjoy herself for a while.

The half hour before Michael was due to come seemed endless. Toni had returned home from school at the usual time and managed to get some homework done. After she grabbed a snack, she soaked in the tub for a long time. She wanted to look especially nice that evening. She also took extra time putting on her eye shadow and lipstick. She never wore blush, feeling that her complexion really didn't need it.

After selecting what she would be wearing, she dressed and then went out to the living room. Her parents were watching TV, but she couldn't keep her mind on the program. With every minute that passed, she became more nervous.

Toni decided to go upstairs to the bathroom to check her hair. The house she lived in was over a hundred years old, but it was warm and cozy, with ample room for the family. The downstairs had a living room, dining room, kitchen, and den, which had been converted into Toni's room when the need arose. There was also a front and back porch. On the upper level, there was a master bedroom, two more bedrooms, and a bath. The house also had an attic that you entered by climbing a stepladder. Toni loved going up there. It was full of vintage clothing she loved to go through.

When Toni got to the second floor, she headed down the hall to the bathroom in the back. After spending about ten minutes in the bathroom, she went into her parents' room to examine herself in their full-length mirror. She was a lovely girl with deep-brown eyes and auburn hair. She had very fair skin, which she knew she got from her mother's side of the family.

As she gazed at her appearance in the mirror, she felt satisfied with what she saw. She stood five feet four and had an average body type. She was wearing dark slacks and a big lightweight sweater she had borrowed from her aunt for the evening.

When the doorbell rang, Toni heard her mother greet Michael. She called up to her, "Toni, dear, your date's here." She was fortunate to have such loving parents.

"I'll be down in a sec, Mom." She took a deep breath and said, "Well, here goes!"

As Toni descended the stairs, she heard her parents speaking with Michael.

"Oh, here you are, dear!" her mother exclaimed. "We were just chatting with Michael."

Toni smiled at Michael and said hello. He returned the smile and the greeting.

"Well," he said lightly, "I guess we should be on our way."

Toni agreed, and they headed for the door.

"Don't be later than midnight, Toni," her father added.

She nodded, and they left.

"Your parents are nice," Michael commented.

"Thanks."

It was a beautiful autumn evening in Minnesota. The trees had already turned and dropped their leaves, which covered the lawns in hues of different colors.

Indian summer had indeed found its way to St. Paul that evening. Toni felt giddy, as if it were a lovely summer night. She was glad to be out. Michael's voice interrupted her thoughts. "I thought we could get a pizza and then catch the flick at the drive-in."

"Sure, that's fine," she agreed happily.

They chatted on about their lives as they drove to Carboni's, a popular teen hangout. Michael told Toni that his father was a lawyer and his mom was a housewife. From what he said, Toni gathered that he and his father didn't get along too well, and when she asked, he agreed.

"My dad is very straight-laced. He had a hard time getting to where he is and expects his kids to be the same. My sister was happy to leave for college because of that."

"He wants you to be a lawyer?" Toni queried.

"Not necessarily a lawyer, but some kind of professional. It's like he has my life all mapped out for me and never bothered to ask me what I wanted."

"And your mom, what is she like?"

"Oh, she's great!" When he spoke of her, his eyes shone. "She's full of fun! I love her very much."

Toni was surprised at his honesty, feeling it was a unique quality in a male.

"She sounds wonderful," she sighed. "I'd like to meet her."

At that, Michael seemed to stiffen a little.

"Is there anything wrong?" she asked in a worried tone.

"No, nothing," he replied, but the tone of his voice revealed that there was.

When they arrived at Carboni's, they ordered a large pizza with everything on it and talked about school. Michael was involved with the Drama Club, and he was also on the basketball team. Toni mentioned her split schedule, which he hadn't been aware of.

"You leave school at eleven thirty?" He seemed surprised to learn that.

"Uh-huh," she replied. "Then I take the bus to St. Paul Vocational and Technical."

"Why do you do that?"

"I'm interested in sewing," she said in between bites of pizza. "No, actually, I'm interested in being a fashion designer."

"Oh, you are?"

"I can't remember when I wasn't designing an outfit for someone in the family. I really love to create. And you, what do you want?"

He paused for a moment as if he weren't sure whether to tell her or not.

"I want to be an architect. I love to build things. When I was a kid, I had a great building set. I'd spend hours working with it. Well, I guess that's what I want." His face grew solemn.

"What's stopping you?" she probed gently.

"To tell you the truth, my grades aren't so good. I sort of goofed off in my junior year, and even though I've been trying to raise my average, it's hard."

"That's why your dad's been giving you a hard time?"

Michael shifted nervously for a moment. "Yeah. He wants me to start college right after high school, and I don't want to. I want to work for a while. I really want to see what it's like out there in the real world."

Toni sensed that there was more to why Michael didn't want to go to college but felt she shouldn't ask, having just met him.

"What type of work are you interested in?"

"I was thinking of construction." He smiled faintly. "I have a friend, and his dad owns a construction company. He said he'd give me a job after I graduated."

"That's really the same kind of work, isn't it?" Toni observed.

"Well, yeah, I guess so. I never really thought of it that way."

With that, they finished their pizza, and as they left Carboni's, Michael put his arm around her and commented, "Boy, time really flies with you."

Toni laughed at his remark. She realized she felt really good. It was as if she could say anything to him. She felt as comfortable with Michael as she did with her own family.

When they reached the drive-in, Michael went for soda, and Toni thought about their evening so far. She liked him. He had many positive qualities: warmth, honesty, sincerity, and a good sense of humor. He was definitely someone she would like to get to know better. He left her with a warm glow. Thoughts of college popped into her head, but she immediately dismissed her worries and decided to enjoy the evening.

When Michael returned from the refreshment stand, he said lightly, "Hey, you don't have to sit all the way over there!" Toni blushed, and Michael laughed at her shyness. "I don't bite, you know," he teased. Toni laughed nervously and moved over next to him. He put his arm around her, and they became absorbed in the movie.

When the film was over, Michael suggested going to Minnehaha Falls. Toni thought that was a great idea. As they drove to the falls, they were both silent but filled with a wonderful sense of peace.

Michael parked the car, and they walked to the falls. It was too dark to see them well, but they could hear the rumble of the water as it cascaded off the rocks. This was a very special place to Toni. She remembered as a child trying to climb the wall surrounding them, but she was never tall enough to do so. Her father would lift her up onto his shoulders so that she could view this breathtaking wonder of nature.

Michael's voice broke the silence. "Toni, I ..." His voice trailed off.

"You don't have to say anything, Michael," she whispered, her heart pounding with anticipation.

"But I want to," he interjected. "I can't remember feeling so good about someone in a long time. I feel so comfortable with you, as if I've known you forever." He pulled her close to him and folded his arms around her. "I really like you," he said softly.

"I really like you too—a lot!"

Toni could feel her heart beating frantically as his lips covered hers. It was almost as loud as the rumble of the falls.

When they drove up to her house, she was sorry the evening was over. It had just disappeared, though she wanted it to go on forever.

"Can I see you again?" Michael asked hopefully as he walked her to the door.

"I'd like that," she said eagerly. As he turned to leave, Toni called out to him, "Michael, didn't you forget something?"

He looked a bit perplexed and didn't answer. She answered her own question. "Didn't you forget to kiss me good night?"

This time, Michael felt awkward. He bent down and his lips softly touched hers. "Good night, Toni."

"Good night." She smiled as she turned to put her key in the lock.

CHAPTER 6

*M*ichael quietly closed the front door so as not to wake his parents and he crept across the living room floor, heading for the stairs.

"Michael," his mother's voice called out to him.

"Mom!" His eyes lit up. "What are you doing up so late?"

"Hi, sweetie!" she greeted her son. "I couldn't sleep. It's just one of those nights when my mind is wide awake." She changed the subject. "How was your date?"

"Great." Michael sighed as he plopped down into the armchair. His parents' home was very nice, a modern house equipped with a fireplace, bar, a rec room on the lower level, and a swimming pool. The furniture was also modern, and the kitchen had all the latest appliances.

"That's really nice, honey," Michael's mother said cheerfully. She knew that he had been going steady with Terri but had thought things weren't going too well between them.

"I met a wonderful girl!" Michael said enthusiastically. "Boy, she's everything I ever wanted, all rolled up in one."

"That's good news, honey. What's her name?"

"Her name is Toni. I met her at school. She's in my English class."

"Honey," Michael's mother said hesitantly, "I hate to put a damper on things, but aren't you still going with Terri?"

Michael sighed heavily and said, "Things haven't been too good between Terri and me for a long time."

"I sensed that, but you can't treat her like that. If you really like this new girl, then you better tell Terri before the whole thing backfires on you."

Apprehension filled Michael's face. "How would Toni find out about Terri? They don't even know each other or live in the same neighborhood. Terri's a junior, and Toni's a senior."

"I don't know, honey," Michael's mother replied, "but things like this have a way of backfiring when you least expect it. You wouldn't want to start out a new relationship with someone you liked, based on lies, would you?" she asked.

Michael readily agreed. "No, Mom. You're right. I have to tell Terri, and right away!"

When Toni walked into her trig class on Monday morning, she was floating on air. Her happiness was so apparent that a classmate asked, "Hey, Toni, you must have had some weekend!"

She looked at Sheryl and smiled. "Oh, hi, Sheryl. Yeah, I did. I met a really nice guy."

She wondered why she hadn't seen Michael in class that morning. Maybe he overslept. Carol broke her train of thought. "What's this lover boy's name?" she asked.

"Michael," Toni murmured dreamily.

"Oh, yeah?" Sheryl asked. "Small world! My best friend, Terri, her boyfriend's name is Michael too."

"Really?" Toni probed. "What's his last name?"

The teacher entered the room just as Sheryl said, "Jameson. His name is Michael Jameson."

Toni froze. She opened her textbook and acted as if she was reading, to avoid Sheryl's eyes. Hers burned with anger. She managed to stammer something to her about the last name being different and acted as if she had to study.

Fury filled her heart. How dare he lie to her? How could he do that? No wonder he asked her out on Friday rather than Saturday. He was probably out with Sheryl's friend on Saturday. She wanted to kill him! To play with her feelings like that was something she wouldn't stand for.

Toni was so upset, she couldn't concentrate on the lesson. She had an important test coming up and would have to borrow someone's notes in order to pass.

When the day was finally over, she went to her locker and collected her things. She wanted to get home as soon as possible, her feelings of deception quickly turning to misery.

The bus took forever. When it finally deposited her at her stop an hour later, she almost ran the last two blocks home.

When Toni arrived home, she greeted her mother and brother and said she would be studying the whole evening and didn't want to be disturbed if anyone called.

"Oh, does that mean Michael also?" Tim queried.

"It means everyone," she said sharply and disappeared into her room.

Her mother and brother exchanged glances.

"I wonder what happened to her?" Tim asked. Her mom shrugged.

Toni opened her bedroom door and collapsed on the bed. She felt totally exhausted and not in the mood to do anything.

The phone rang a few minutes later, and Tim answered. He came to her door and said, "Hey, sis, it's Michael."

"I said I didn't want to be disturbed!" she screamed angrily.

"Okay, okay. Don't take it out on me," he replied, annoyed by her reaction.

The week seemed to drag on for Toni. By the time Thursday came, she wished it was already Saturday so she could sleep in. She was feeling exhausted and needed some emotional refreshment.

When Toni returned home from school that afternoon, Tim approached her. "I don't understand you," he began. "I thought you liked that guy, Michael."

She didn't respond, and Tim continued, "He's called six times, and frankly, I'm tired of taking messages for you. Why don't you talk to him?"

Toni listened silently to what her brother had to say.

"You're not helping matters by avoiding him."

She realized that he was right and said she'd speak to him the next time he called.

Later that evening, Michael called. Toni dreaded answering the phone but at the same time wanted to get the whole mess resolved one way or another.

"Toni, why have you been avoiding me?" he said heatedly. "I'm becoming good friends with Tim. I don't know how I couldn't. I speak with him every time I call."

There was silence at the other end of the line.

"Will you at least tell me what's wrong?"

"Oh, come on!" Toni said impatiently. "You're going to tell me you don't know what's wrong?"

"No, I don't, and I'm not in the mood for playing games."

"Okay," she said angrily, "her name is Terri. I believe you've been introduced. In fact, you know her so well, she's your steady girlfriend."

Michael winced as he heard the harshness in Toni's voice. "I was going to tell you," he said in a small voice. "Honest, I was."

"When, Michael?" she asked, hardened by his deception. "After ten Friday nights? Why did you lie to me? Why didn't you tell me the truth from the start? I really don't know what type of relationship you and Terri have. Maybe she's used to your lies, but I won't take it for one minute!"

"Please listen to me," Michael pleaded. "I was going to tell you as soon as I broke up with her. I was planning on telling her last Saturday, but I just didn't get around to it."

By this time, Toni's anger had dissipated, and all she felt was sadness. She said firmly, "When you get around to it, give me a call, and not before."

Tears filled Toni's eyes as she hung up the phone. As for Michael on the other end, he was feeling pretty sad and very angry at himself.

Why didn't he tell Terri it was over between them? Did he still care for her? Or was he frightened of what the future held? No, it was neither of those things.

Boy, he really blew it! He had finally found the kind of girl he needed, and then he lied to her. He thought of his mother's advice and didn't understand why he hadn't followed it. He'd have to get his act together and hoped Toni would give him another chance.

Two long weeks had passed since Toni spoke with Michael. Her feeling of sadness was still with her, but unusual for her young age, she sensed that if given enough time, that would pass, and she'd forget about him altogether.

English class was especially difficult now with Michael seated so close to her, but she tried hard not to glance his way and concentrate on the lesson. Most of the time it worked, but a few times he turned to look at her, and she caught his glance. She quickly looked away but was always left with an uncomfortable feeling.

Friday morning, Toni was coming out of school to go to St. Paul Tech when she heard a car honk. She glanced at it and saw a beautiful red Mustang parked at the curb. Then she looked away and started heading toward the bus stop, but the car honked again. The driver lowered the window, and Toni realized it was Michael. She hesitated a minute and then decided to walk over to the car.

"Hi," she said flatly. She couldn't help but wonder about the car. "Is this your car?"

"Yeah. I had my dad's car the last time I saw you." He continued, "Can I give you a lift to school?"

"Aren't you supposed to be in school?" she asked.

"Yeah, but I asked my mom to write me an early excuse note. Why don't you get in?"

They drove along for a mile or so, and then Michael pulled the car over and parked.

"Will you just hear me out? That's all I ask, and then you can do what you want to do." She nodded in agreement.

"I should have broken up with Terri the night after I saw you. In fact, I had a talk with my mom, and she said the same thing, but it seems like lately everyone is telling me what to do, and I have to move at my own pace, not everyone else's!" he concluded.

"Your dad is telling you what to do, Michael. He's not everyone," Toni said flatly.

He looked away for a moment and then said shyly, "I think I could care for you. I know we just met, but right from the start, it felt ..." He hesitated, trying to find the right word. "It just felt good! Please give me a chance to make up for this."

"I'm not into changing people like a lot of my friends," Toni began. "I'm not selfish and expect people to be what I want them to be. I'm more the accepting type, but I do need to know that I can trust the person I'm with, and I can't if you lie to me."

Michael reached for her hand and held it tightly. Toni looked intently into his eyes, waiting for his reaction.

"I blew it." He laughed nervously. "I know I did, but I'm asking you for a second chance to make up for what I did. I won't beg. I'm too proud for that, but I feel that there's something special between us, and we'd be really silly if we let it go now."

Toni looked away because she sensed she was close to tears. She held them back and turned to him. "I think you're right. We do have something special. Maybe someday you'll know why you acted the way you did, and we can talk about it." Michael bent over and kissed her.

Soft, quiet emotions swept through her. She knew he was

feeling the same things—wonderful, delightful feelings that she, at her young age, had never experienced.

As their lips parted, Michael gave Toni a small peck on the nose and said, "I better get you to school. I'll be waiting for you when you come out."

Toni smiled and said, "Really?"

"We have two weeks to make up for, and I want to start tonight."

When he dropped her off, Toni smiled as he drove away. She wasn't sure if what she had done was right, but this had nothing to do with her common sense. Her heart was in complete control, and she had to go where it wanted to take her.

CHAPTER 7

s the snow covered the ground, Michael and Toni's love grew stronger. They had found in each other a deep sense of happiness.

Winter in Minnesota was something to behold. With the cold weather came mountains of snow, which would turn to rain, and huge icicles would hang from the trees, creating a winter wonderland. The lakes and ponds would freeze over, enabling people to participate in winter sports such as ice fishing and skating. The hills would soon be covered with snow for sledding and tobogganing, and people of all ages would be enjoying themselves.

The cold became so intense at times, sometimes dropping to ten below, that one would have to dress in many layers to keep warm.

The month of January featured the St. Paul Winter Carnival. A feeling of gaiety overtook the city. A medallion would be hidden somewhere in the city, and clues would be published daily in the local paper. The winner would win a cash prize of a thousand dollars.

Also, a snow queen would be crowned to reign over the parade. The whole city felt like a carnival.

During that time period, Michael introduced Toni to his closest friends, Jason and Tracy. Jason was a natural comic, always cracking jokes. He had Michael and Toni in stitches whenever they spent time together. Tracy was also full of fun. She had a zest for living that was hard to surpass. She wanted to do everything once, and if she liked it, twice. Tracy was immediately drawn to this happy couple who were so suited for each other.

Michael told Toni that Jason and Tracy had been together since junior high and had plans to attend the University of Minnesota after graduation and, if funds would allow, to marry. Jason hoped to be a doctor, and Tracy had plans to be a lawyer.

The four of them spent many weekends together, going to movies, concerts, ice-skating, bowling, and other teenage activities. Toni could see the genuine affection Michael had for them and was happy that he had such loving friends. Toni had always been very studious and never really had time to make close friends. Also, because of her shy personality, she found it hard to make friends easily.

Christmas was soon upon them, and Toni was invited to Michael's home for Christmas Eve dinner. She had an opportunity to meet Michael's parents, whom she found to be charming.

"Michael tells me you have plans to be a designer, Toni," Michael's father said, full of curiosity.

"Yes, that's true. I plan to go to college."

"Well, I've been trying to encourage Michael to go to college also, but I don't seem to be getting anywhere."

"Dad," Michael said, exasperated.

"Okay," his father said, "I'll drop it."

Toni saw Michael tense up immediately. She knew the problems he had with his father and saw how both of them were trying hard to be on their best behavior.

The evening went quite well. Toni had time to chat alone with Michael's mother, whom she found to be very personable.

"Michael loves you very much, Toni."

She was taken aback by his mother's sincerity but nevertheless responded. "I know. I love him too."

"I hope you're going off to college doesn't ruin things for you," she remarked.

"Maybe I'll be able to convince him to come along."

"Yes, maybe you will," she said confidently.

On a Saturday evening in February, Michael and Toni went to the drive-in. When they arrived there, Michael put his arm around her and drew her to him. He kissed her hungrily, and some moments later, when they parted, Toni felt breathless with desire for him. He drew her close to him and held her tightly.

"I'm crazy about you, baby," he said huskily. "Oh, God, Toni. I don't know how much more of this I can take. I love you and need to feel you close to me."

"I am close to you, Michael," she whispered.

"You know what I mean," he insisted. "I need to make love to you."

"I don't know if I'm ready for that."

"Toni, please," he implored. "I need to be deep inside you!"

Toni buried her head in his chest and said, "I need that too, Michael, but where are we going to go?"

"We'll work those things out." His lips found the nape of her neck and covered her with small, tender kisses.

As was their custom, Toni's parents went out every Saturday night. Her brother, Tim, was never around either, as he usually spent lots of time with his friends. Toni arranged with Michael to come over the following Saturday night. Because her bedroom had a door leading onto the front porch, it would be easy for him to enter without being noticed.

That evening, Michael parked his car a few blocks away from Toni's home, so her parents wouldn't spot it. Suddenly, he was hit with a real case of nerves; why, he couldn't understand. He loved this girl very much. In the past six months, he had been happier than he could ever remember. He realized that was the source of his anxiety. She wasn't just any girl but someone very important to him, and he wanted everything to go well. In the two years he had spent with Terri, they made love several times, but he didn't have the feelings for her that he did for Toni. He was beginning to feel something that he hadn't been aware of—a feeling of needing someone more than one could imagine, that when they hurt, you hurt; a vulnerability he had never allowed himself to feel for anyone. He was scared.

When the realization hit him of what he was feeling, he was tempted to turn around and go home, but he had come too far for that. His lovely, sweet Toni was here waiting for him, and he had to go to her.

As Michael approached Toni's house, he remembered she told him she would leave the side door open, and he just had to knock. He did as she instructed, and for what seemed like a century, he waited, until a light went on in the room and Toni came to the door. When she opened the door, he noticed the room was illuminated by candlelight. It made her look like an angel in her lovely white gown. The candle caught the transparency of the gown, and he gasped at the loveliness of her body.

Toni blushed as his eyes moved up and down her body, and she reached for his hand and ushered him into the room. He could sense she was nervous, and they sat on the bed for a while holding hands.

"You look beautiful," he murmured softly to her and she smiled. The gown she was wearing was one of her nicest ones. The top had a border of blue lace, and it was cut in such a way that it revealed her cleavage. From beneath her breasts, gores of material hung down to create a lovely, flowing skirt.

After a while, Toni suggested that Michael undress, and she slipped under the covers. She watched him with a growing excitement that she had never experienced before. As he removed his clothing, he exposed a young, muscular chest. His buttocks were also muscular and full. As her eyes trailed down to his manliness, she gasped, breathless with emotion at the greatness of it. Her Michael, indeed, had the body of a Greek god. His skin shone in the candlelight as he carefully laid his clothing over a chair and then slowly got into bed next to her.

"Your feet are freezing!" Toni exclaimed. They both laughed, and their nervousness quickly dissipated.

Michael leaned over and gently kissed her, and she trembled as his hands gently ran through her hair, caressing every strand. She let out a sigh of sweet desire. As his hands moved skillfully across her body, she responded with little moans that expressed her pleasure. His lips moved down her face, to her neck, and then to her beautiful, creamy breasts, which were aching for his touch. They responded to his lips with enthusiasm, becoming rigid in his mouth as he sucked each one.

As inexperienced as Toni was, she loved him and wanted to please him. Her hand moved down his body until she found his wondrous organ. He gave a start when he felt her fondling him gently and stroking his bulging organ.

With every kiss, every caress, Toni's passion increased until it was at a point where she could control it no longer. She moved her hand over Michael's manhood, and it grew harder with every stroke. His mouth found its way down to Toni's stomach until it reached her fiery core. His tongue skillfully found its way into that luscious core and licked her slowly until she shook violently with desire. Finally, when she could stand it no longer, she pleaded with him to enter her. His body moved on top of her, and he lay there covering her with deep, gentle kisses as his hardness searched for her below. It was like a tempting velvet trap—so hot and wet—just waiting to be entered.

A moment later, he answered her pleas, and she let out a scream of excruciating pain. With every thrust, it became less painful, and intense pleasure took its place. Deeper and harder Michael pushed himself inside as her womanliness opened itself like a rose to sunshine to accommodate him. She was filled with a feeling of ecstasy that was so overwhelming, it seemed as if she would explode. A moment later, Toni's body gave way to a pleasure she had never before experienced. Michael soon after joined her in that wondrous rapture.

As they lay in quiet afterglow, entwined in each other's arms, they were filled with such a deep sense of contentment.

Their love had been made complete. Michael kissed Toni's eyes, face, ears, and nose and whispered softly to her, "I never knew I could love anyone the way I do you."

She smiled and held him closer to her. He completed her life by filling a void she never knew she'd had until she met him. He was the other part she was missing. How lucky they were to love the way they did.

CHAPTER 8

The months passed quickly for Toni, filled with school-work, Michael, and her varied hobbies. April was soon upon her, keeping her busy designing and sewing Easter outfits.

Loving Michael was something Toni couldn't put into words. They had made love several times since that first night, and every time was just as wonderful as the first. Michael's parents had gone away a few weekends, and they took advantage of their absence by making mad, passionate love in front of the fireplace. They were also given permission to use his parents' cabin, which was located a few hours away from St. Paul. They would pass whole Saturdays, from morning to evening, locked in their passionate lovemaking.

Toni found it hard to imagine a life without Michael, but thoughts of school would filter in to disrupt her peace. She had already applied to several excellent fashion schools in New York and was accepted to three of them. She decided on Fashion Institute of Technology for its reputation and success rate for students.

Toni hadn't discussed school with Michael too much. She hoped and prayed that when the time came, he would be agreeable to her suggestion of coming with her. Not for a moment did she think she would go without him.

Graduation was rapidly approaching—just a few weeks away—and Toni had so much to do. As the days grew warmer, Michael and Toni took long drives out to some of the state parks in the St. Paul area.

They would ramble through the woods, taking in the sights, smells, and sounds of Mother Nature at her best. The sunlight glistened through the trees as a gentle breeze shook the leaves, and the birds responded with their own melodic tune. The variety of trees was endless, and the couple enjoyed collecting and identifying the leaves.

Toni's parents would always shop on Saturday afternoons. After they would leave, Michael would come over, and they'd spend a few hours making love as the lazy afternoon sun showered them with warmth.

On one particular Saturday in June, Toni and Michael had just finished making love when he pulled out a small box.

"Here!" He motioned for her to take it. "This is for you."

"But what is it?" Toni asked, hoping it wasn't what she thought.

Michael smiled tenderly. "Why don't you open it and see."

Toni opened the box to find inside a lovely ring with a small emerald in the center, surrounded by diamonds.

Toni gasped as she realized what was happening. "Michael, what is this?"

Michael took the ring from the box and put it on her finger. He smiled and kissed her as she sat there gasping.

"Michael, please don't play games with me!" she protested. "What does this mean?"

Michael seemed very nervous and looked away for a moment. In all the time Toni had known him, she couldn't recall his reacting this way. He finally said, "I love you very much, and I'm asking you to marry me."

"Michael—" Her voice faltered.

"You don't have to say anything now," he cut in.

"Please listen to me," she pleaded with him. "I love you too. You have made me very happy, and *yes,* I'll marry you, but please come to New York with me."

Apprehension filled her face as she saw his reaction.

"New York?" he raged. "How long have you known about this? You've been leading me on all these months!" he screamed as his face reddened with fury.

Toni couldn't believe what she was hearing. She was seeing a side of Michael she never knew existed.

As he bent down to put his shoes on, she reached for his arm, and he pushed her hand away.

"Michael, please," Toni pleaded, "please just talk to me. We can work this out. I know we can. Just give us a chance."

"Work what out?" he snarled. "You're planning on flying out of my life. Is that what you call working it out?"

"Michael, please—" A feeling of dread filled her.

Michael stalked off the porch and down the front stairs. Toni heard him get into his car and drive away. She looked down at the ring on her finger, and tears filled her eyes, running down her cheeks.

She didn't know how long she lay there on the bed sobbing.

It seemed like hours. When she heard her parents' voices, she sat up quickly and ran upstairs to the bathroom. She didn't want them to see her that way. She quickly splashed water on her face.

What had she done? Why didn't she discuss school with him earlier? Why, dear Lord, did she wait so long?

She needed to get out of the house and decided to take a walk. She walked for what felt like hours, reflecting on why she hadn't told him. She thought they would have the whole summer together, and she'd be able to convince him to come to New York with her. She didn't understand why he was so adamant about staying in St. Paul, why he became so angry when she told him of her plans.

When Toni returned that night, her mother knew right away something was wrong. She came over to her and hugged her, and Toni told her what had happened.

Summer passed very slowly. After graduation, Toni found employment in the office at St. Paul Tech. She thought it would help her stop mooning over Michael and she'd be able to save some money for college. She couldn't believe that six weeks had passed since she and Michael broke up, and not a word from him. Tracy told Toni that he was working in construction, but that was all she had heard. She tried speaking with him several times, but when she called, his mother said he wasn't there. Finally, she decided to speak with her about the problem, and Mrs. Jameson agreed that Michael was acting very funny. He wouldn't even discuss it with her but only insisted angrily that he wouldn't go to New York.

"What can I do?" Toni asked. "I love Michael, but I'm not going to stay in St. Paul to become a wife and mother and regret that decision for the rest of my life. I want more than that."

"Honey, you have to do what you feel is right, but I know my son, and as much as he loves you, he's just as stubborn. I'll try to work on him, but I won't make any promises. I love you, Toni, and since Michael met you, I hoped you two would marry, but if you want an education, go get it, and think of marriage later."

"Yes, but will Michael be there later?"

"I don't know, honey," said Mrs. Jameson doubtfully.

The conversation didn't leave Toni feeling any better. Why did she have to choose between Michael and a career? This was the 1970s, not the '40s. Things were changing for women, but obviously they were just the same for men. She wanted them both. The more she thought about it, the more outraged she became.

"All right!" she said to herself adamantly. "If I have to give up Michael, I will, but it isn't fair. It just isn't fair!"

At the airport, Toni sat with her parents and brother, waiting to board. She kept looking around, hoping that Michael would appear at the last moment and say he was going with her. Her parents and brother knew what she was going through, how much Michael meant to her. Her rage, by this time, had turned to remorse. She really didn't know how she was going to pull this off, but many weeks had passed since she last saw Michael. She felt that if she could live without him all that time, she could also do so while she was in school. After school, she'd come home, and they'd be married. It was only two years. It already seemed like an eternity.

Toni heard the announcement over the loudspeaker that the plane was ready to board. She hugged and kissed her family and started heading toward the jet way. As she walked, a horrible feeling of emptiness invaded her. It was the very worst feeling she had ever felt in her life. She thought that at any moment, she was going to faint but managed to find her seat before that happened.

As the plane taxied down the runway, a feeling of nausea came over her. For a moment, she wanted to run off the plane, find Michael, and tell him she'd marry him—but she couldn't do it. What kind of life would they have if they both felt he stopped her from doing what she wanted? She concentrated on closing her eyes, but large tears welled up and made their way under her lashes, down her cheeks.

Michael stood at the observation window, watching her plane as it took off. Two years was a lifetime, but he hoped he could wait until she returned to him and became his wife. He held the ring in his hand. She had returned it, along with a letter asking him to wait for her. She again pleaded for him to join her in New York. A combination of anxiety and hurt filled his heart. He couldn't go to New York with her! Why couldn't she understand that? He just couldn't!

Toni wasn't the only one crying on that somber day in early September.

CHAPTER 9

When Toni returned to St. Paul, on her first day home, she made a lot of progress. She had managed to get a lot of her things unpacked, and her furniture had arrived the day before. She loved her apartment. Her mom was right—it was perfect for her. It had a combination living/dining area off the main entrance, a walk-in kitchen, one small bedroom that she intended to use as her workroom, and a large master bedroom. It had been recently painted in colors her mom chose for her. The bedroom was done in her favorite color, powder blue, just like her bedroom in her parents' home. The kitchen was done in orange with yellow accessories. She figured if the sunlight didn't wake her up, her brightly painted kitchen definitely would. The living/dining area was done in beige and brown, and her small workroom was done in violet. Two of the walls were covered with pegboards to hold her many design tools and patterns. The room was modestly furnished with a drawing table, a sewing machine, and a small dresser for miscellaneous supplies.

The phone rang just as Toni was putting her dishes away.

"Hello," Toni said brightly.

The voice on the other end of the line laughed. "Toni!"

She immediately knew who it was. "Jason!" She giggled. Jason was such a comic—so full of life. He didn't take too much seriously. She loved him and Tracy very much.

"Well, kid, how's it going? Getting settled in your new abode?"

"I love it here," Toni responded emphatically. "It's just perfect for me and very convenient to everything."

"I figured you'd like it. You know your mom called Tracy and me when she found the place. She wanted to make sure it was your style. We gave it a going-over and told her okay." He changed his tone to a more serious one. "Listen, sweetie, sorry about what happened at the airport," he said. "I thought for sure he'd show."

Toni said solemnly, "He was there, Jason. I saw him walk away."

"I figured he'd be there. I told him what time your flight was. I guess he got cold feet."

"How is he? What does he look like now?" she asked, anxious to know.

"Oh, he hasn't changed much. He's older, but then we all are." Jason chuckled. "He was really surprised when I told him you were coming home. Maybe that's why he stayed away. He hasn't had time to digest the whole thing."

"I want to see him very badly," Toni said impatiently. "How long is he going to make me wait?"

Jason tried to calm her down. "He'll come around, honey. Just give him time. Hey, Tracy wants to speak with you."

Toni spoke with Tracy for a few minutes and then hung up the phone. All of a sudden, she felt weary and decided to leave the rest of the unpacking for another day.

Two weeks had passed since Toni's return to St. Paul. She had fallen into a routine at Shapiro's Swimwear. She loved her new job and realized she was fortunate to continue in swimwear. Her extensive training in swimsuit design had paid off. Mr. Shapiro seemed pleased and took time to explain things to her. She felt she had a sound future with the firm.

On the bus ride home, Toni read the paper and wondered when Michael would contact her. The thought of contacting him had crossed her mind, but she decided against it. The ball was in his court. She had returned to St. Paul for one reason alone: to be with him. It was his turn to approach her. She would just have to wait patiently until he called.

The weather in early autumn was beautiful. Many of the trees had changed colors and discarded their leaves as they waited for winter to give them a new coat. As a child, Toni recalled piling up all the leaves on the block with the neighborhood children and then jumping into them. The temperature was perfect for her. If she had her way, she would prefer autumn all year long.

Toni pulled off her shoes and plopped down on the couch. Work was very busy these past few days, and she enjoyed this part of the day more than any other.

She closed her eyes for a few minutes and was brought back to consciousness by the ringing of the phone.

Probably Mom, she thought as she rose to answer it.

"Hello," she said warmly and froze as she recognized the voice on the other end of the line.

"Toni?" he asked shyly. It was Michael! The words stuck in her throat.

"Toni," he repeated, "are you there?"

"Yes. Yes, I'm here," she stammered. How was it that this man always made her feel so awkward? "I'm just surprised to hear your voice."

There was silence on the other end, and then he asked, "How are you?"

"I'm okay," she responded brightly. "How are you?"

"Fine. Jason told me you returned."

"Jason?" she asked. Her heart pounded furiously. "Yes. Well, there was nothing holding me in California, and I was anxious to see my family." She bit her tongue, hoping he hadn't detected her fib.

"Well, I'd like to see you," he remarked. "Do you have plans for dinner tonight?"

"No, I haven't made any."

"Good! Can I pick you up around seven?"

"Sure! Fine," she agreed.

As she hung up the telephone, Toni realized she was numb. In an hour, Michael would be here—in her apartment. After all the times she thought of seeing him, she never thought it would be like this. But after reflecting on it, Toni realized it was just like him to call, out of the blue, and ask to see her. She panicked as she wondered what she should wear. She decided on blue jeans and a velvet top and drew a hot bath, intending to soak until her nerves were quieted.

When the doorbell rang, Toni slowly rose to answer it. She didn't want to seem overly anxious. Oh, how silly she was being! This was Michael, the boy she fell in love with in high school. But then she recalled all the things that had happened in between: her graduating from college; the news of his marriage to Terri; her decision not to return to St. Paul and to settle in California; Noel.

The doorbell rang for the second time, just as she reached to open it.

"Hi." He stood there, dressed in a brown sweater and tan slacks. Her eyes feasted on him. She had waited so long to see him, and now he stood before her. A moment of silence went by, and he finally said, "May I come in?" Toni nodded and he entered the room. That old feeling of awkwardness was overcoming her again.

"You look great." He smiled. "You took off some weight, right?"

"I guess so," she replied as she motioned him to sit down on the couch. "You haven't changed much, Michael."

But when she looked a little closer, she realized he had. He looked older, tired. She sensed his marriage to Terri hadn't agreed with him.

"Are you ready to go?" he asked.

"Yes," she replied happily. "Where are we going, by the way?"

"They just opened up a new pizza place downtown, and I thought you would like to try it."

Toni smiled as she remembered his fascination with pizza.

As they walked downstairs, Toni noticed Michael's red Mustang parked outside. She recalled all the wonderful evenings they had spent in that car.

He opened the door for her, and she said, "I remember those bucket seats."

He laughed at her with amusement. "You never liked them, did you?"

She shook her head.

They drove downtown in silence. Toni was thinking how good it was to be home and to be with Michael again, but there were questions she had to ask him, things she needed to know.

After they ordered the pizza and Michael devoured half of it, Toni asked, "Are you still in construction?"

"Yeah, I am. I like the work," he said, feeling somehow he had to give her an excuse for his choice of work. "And you," he continued. "You're a designer now." She nodded. "I give you a lot of credit. You set out to do something, and you did it." She smiled as she finished off a piece.

"Congratulations!" Michael went on. "My mom tells me Shapiro's is one of the finest swimwear companies in town."

"The owner is really a nice man." Without pausing, she continued, "Michael, why did you marry Terri?"

Michael was not prepared for the question and almost gagged on his pizza. "You haven't changed much, Toni. You're just as candid as always," he commented. "I don't know. She was always hanging around, and she loved me. I guess I thought I could learn to love her too."

Toni's heart was filled with fear for a moment. Then she said, trembling, with emotion, "I told you I was coming back."

"But then I didn't hear from you for two years, and I thought you got to the big city and forgot all about me."

"But I wrote you," she interjected, "a few weeks after I got there. You must have gotten the letter."

"What letter?" His eyes were full of curiosity. "I never got a letter from you. I would have written back right away."

"Maybe you should ask your mom," Toni answered flatly.

"I will. As soon as I get home," he said.

They spent the rest of the evening on small talk, and as Michael drove her home, Toni was quiet. He walked her to her door, and she asked hesitantly, "Will I see you again?"

He reached out for her hand and squeezed it tightly. "Yes, you will, and I intend to find out what happened to that letter."

When Michael returned home, he dropped his coat on a chair and dialed his parents' number. "Hi, Mom," he said.

"Oh, hi, honey. How are you doing?"

"Okay." He paused for a moment and then said, "I saw Toni tonight."

"Toni?" Michael's mother couldn't contain her excitement. "How is she?"

"She's fine. Just as pretty as ever," he said happily. "Mom, it's been a while, but I want you to think hard and tell me if you remember anything about a letter. I never saw it."

"Well, honey, it was a while ago. Let me sleep on it, and I'll call you tomorrow, if I remember anything."

"Okay, Mom."

"Love you, Michael."

"Me too, Mom."

The following day, Michael's mother called and left a message for him. When he took his lunch break, he returned the call.

"Hi, Mom. Did you remember anything?"

"Yes," she responded. "I seem to recall a letter coming for you from New York. Terri had been coming over a lot during that time, wasn't she? It was right after you got back from the cabin."

"Yes," Michael recalled, "she was."

"If my memory serves me right, Terri saw the letter laying there and said she'd give it to you that evening. I thought it was kind of strange, now that I think of it."

"Well, Mom, I never got it."

"Then you'll have to ask her, son," his mother suggested.

Michael's face was red with rage as he hung up the phone. He put two and two together and had a good idea what happened to that letter. He decided he's call on his ex-wife before going to bed that evening.

When the doorbell rang, Terri was in the kitchen. She reached for a towel to wipe her hands and headed for the door.

"Michael!" she exclaimed with surprise when she opened the door and saw him standing there. "What are you doing here?"

"I have a little unfinished business with you," he said coldly as he walked into the apartment.

"With me?" Terri asked, apprehension filling her face.

"No, with your mother," he responded sarcastically. She had lived with this man long enough to know that she was in for trouble. "It seems a letter disappeared from my house about four years ago, and my mother said you took it to give it to me."

"I have it?" she asked, feigning innocence.

"Don't try my patience," Michael said firmly. "I want it and *now*."

"I don't know what you're talking about."

"Get that damn letter for me *now!*" Michael growled. Terri flinched. She had never seen Michael so angry before. In the years they were married, it took a lot to get him worked up. He was usually very calm.

"I don't have it, Michael."

"What happened to it?"

"I burned it."

"You *what?*"

"I loved you. I would have done anything to win you."

"What did it say?" Michael asked.

"She wanted to come home and marry you."

Michael sat staring at Terri, a stunned look on his face. After the numbness passed, he was filled with fury. "You bitch!" he yelled. "You stopped her from coming home!"

"It was a long time ago, Michael."

"I wanted her. Can't you understand that? She's the only woman I ever wanted."

He stormed out of the house and headed for his car, where he sat shaken for what seemed like hours. When the anger finally passed, he was filled with a deep sense of remorse. He put his head in his hands and didn't even realize he was crying until the tears filled his hands and fell onto the floor.

What would he say to Toni? All those years away from her, thinking she had stopped loving him, when Terri had stopped their happiness from flowering. He drove home in silence.

When Michael got home, he parked his car in front of his apartment and slowly climbed the stairs. He felt as if all the energy had been drained from him. He turned the key in the lock and didn't bother snapping on the light. He found his way to the couch and sat there in silence. All he could think of was four wasted years. How could he ever make up for them? Four years without the only woman he had ever loved! He pulled himself up and headed for the fridge. He found a six-pack in the bottom shelf and consumed it all.

Some hours later, after the drink had forced him into sleep, he woke feeling groggy. Moments later, his conversation with Terri and all the other memories came rushing back. He knew he had to call Toni.

"Hello," Toni said warmly. He loved the sound of her voice.

"I spoke to Terri," he said. "She read it and burned it but remembered certain parts—that you wanted to come home and attend the University of Minnesota Fashion Division so we wouldn't be separated. I don't know what to say."

"Don't say anything right now," she urged him.

"But, Toni, all those wasted years!" Michael's voice was full of exasperation. "We could have been together, and that bitch ruined it for us!"

"That's all in the past now, Michael. We can't bring it back, but," she said hopefully, "we have the present and the future, don't we?"

"Yes, Toni, we do," he said happily.

Her heart soared when she heard his reply.

CHAPTER 10

The following day, the alarm went off at the usual time, and Toni stretched her limbs and then jumped out of bed and went about readying herself for work. An hour later, she headed out the door to catch her bus, and to her surprise, the red Mustang was parked in front of the building. A smile filled her face when she saw Michael.

As he rolled down the window, he said, "Hi, lady! Could you use a ride to work?"

Toni giggled and said, "Sure! But won't you be late?"

"No," he said softly, "I have plenty of time." His eyes were brimming over with tenderness for her.

Toni hopped in the car, and Michael started off. She felt so happy, she thought she would burst. She couldn't recall feeling that way in a very long time.

"How are you doing?" Michael asked.

"Fine." She couldn't help feeling fine. At least the decision she made to return home had proven to be the right one. She did have a chance to be with Michael again.

Michael broke her train of thought by asking, "Are you busy for dinner tonight?"

"It's Tuesday," she replied. "I have to work until 7:00 p.m. and usually just want to go home and collapse." He seemed disappointed but didn't reply. When they arrived at Toni's workplace, he bent over and kissed her tenderly. "Have a nice day."

"You too!"

"I'll call you later," he added and a moment later was gone.

Toni's day flew by. She couldn't help thinking about Michael and how much she loved him. Even though she was extremely busy, thoughts of him would flow into her mind, leaving her with a soft, warm glow. She was glad that the mystery of the letter had been solved, and she pitied Terri. She thought of the adage "what goes around comes around," and Terri would pay in the end. But she already had paid by losing Michael.

A feeling of sadness filled her when she realized that if things had gone differently, she and Michael would have been married, with their love growing deeper as time passed. She preferred not to dwell on the past and thought of the wonderful future they would have together.

Designing bathing suits was very interesting to Toni. The work was very technical and not at all what she expected, but she always had breaks in her day when customers would come to be measured for a swimsuit. She was proud of herself for achieving what she wanted out of life and only hoped that one day Michael would do the same.

When Toni arrived home that evening, it wasn't long before the phone rang and she heard that warm, familiar voice on the other end of the line. "Hi."

"Hi, Michael," she responded.

"How was your day?"

"Very busy, but I loved every minute of it."

"I was wondering, do you think you could get up a half hour earlier than usual?"

"Sure, I suppose so," she replied. "What do you have in mind?"

"There's a cute little place not far from your job. I thought we could have breakfast there together."

"Sounds great to me." As she hung up the phone, she sensed that someone up there was looking out for her.

The following morning, when Toni left her apartment, Michael was waiting at the curb.

"Hi, sweetie!" he greeted her affectionately as she got into the car.

"Hi," she said, delighted that he had used a term of endearment with her. She wasn't expecting miracles, certainly not after four years. Things would probably have to develop slowly, but she hoped that this morning's overture was an indication that he was starting to open up to her.

"I feel great!" Michael exclaimed, his eyes twinkling with warmth.

"Any special reason?" Toni probed.

"I don't know. It's just that since we've been dating, I feel that I've been holding back a part of myself."

"Well, I guess that's normal, considering we haven't seen each other in four years."

"Four years is a long time, isn't it?" Michael queried.

Toni nodded. "I felt it would take a while until we both felt comfortable with each other again. Also, we're not the kids we were then."

"I guess we've both changed," Michael observed, "but my feelings for you haven't."

He reached over to hold her hand and looked intently at her. Her eyes had a glow in them that Michael hadn't seen in a long time. Toni knew they had gone through some rough times but that was behind them.

When they finished breakfast, Michael walked Toni to her building and asked hopefully, "I'll see you tonight?"

"Yes," she said softly. He bent over and kissed her lightly on the lips and then headed for his car.

As the weeks went by, Michael and Toni spent almost every day together. Although they did not speak of their love for each other, it was apparent that it was growing stronger with each passing day.

The couple was getting ready to go out on a Friday night when the phone rang. Toni rose to pick it up and heard the voice on the other end of the line. "Toni, how are you, baby?"

"Jason, it's good to hear from you."

"Same here, lady. Hey, is the big guy there?"

"Sure. We were just about to head out."

Michael took the phone from Toni and chuckled when he heard his friend's voice on the line.

"Hi, Mike. How's life?"

"Life is great, Jason," Michael said. "Hey, what's up with you?"

"Tracy and I found this great place downtown. They serve

the best pizza *and* they have a dance floor. Hey, man, we haven't seen you guys for a while. Why don't you join us?"

"Sounds good to me. Let me check with Toni." He asked Toni, and she thought it was a fine idea.

"Why don't you meet us there in, let's say, forty-five minutes?"

"Okay," Michael said, "see you then."

When Michael and Toni arrived at the club, it took a while to locate their friends. It was packed with people standing at the bar, seated around the dance floor, and dancing. The smoke was so thick that Toni had to wave it away as she entered the room. Finally, they found Jason and Tracy and slowly worked their way to their table.

"Hey! How are you guys?" Jason shouted through the noise, with a broad smile on his face that matched his twinkling eyes.

"We are great!" Michael responded, matching his enthusiasm. The four of them exchanged hugs and kisses and settled into their seats. Tracy and Toni chatted away while the guys filled each other in on their recent activities.

Memories of the good times Toni had spent with these three people came to mind. All of the wonderful things she and Michael had done with them in high school came back.

The evening passed, filled with good feelings for each other. Then a record came on that propelled Toni back to the late '60s. She looked at Michael, who was laughing with Jason about something. When he heard the song, he said something to Jason, picked himself up, and stood before her.

"May I have this dance, lovely lady?" His eyes were filled with tenderness for her.

She teased at him in a light, comical tone. "You certainly may, kind sir."

They worked their way to the dance floor, and Michael pulled her to him and held her closely as their bodies blended with the beat of the music. His arms were wrapped tightly around her back and hers around his neck. He pulled her a little closer so that her head was resting on his shoulder.

As they danced, they became filled with emotion for each other. They were so completely mesmerized by each other, it was as if they were all alone in the loud, dark club. Michael looked at Toni, and suddenly his lips were on hers, kissing her with a deep longing and tenderness.

"Let's go, honey," he whispered huskily, and she nodded in agreement.

They made their way back to the table and told Jason and Tracy they were going to leave. They didn't protest. Somehow, they sensed the two wanted to be alone. As Toni and Michael headed toward the door, Jason and Tracy exchanged a knowing glance, and he reached to squeeze his wife's hand.

As they drove back to Toni's apartment, she hoped and prayed that the night wouldn't end with just a kiss. She needed so much more than that. They approached the building, and Michael pulled into the parking lot instead of dropping her out front.

"May I come up?" She could hear his heart beating as he asked the question.

"Yes," she said simply, her heart matching the beat of his as they ascended the stairs together. She found her key, and within seconds, they were in the apartment, holding each other.

Michael kissed her lips with a tenderness that made her tremble with longing for him. Then he whispered, "I never stopped loving you. Not for a day. Not for a minute."

Tears sprang to Toni's eyes and ran down her cheeks when she heard the words that her soul had been deprived of for so very long.

"Honey!" Michael said, alarmed. "What's wrong?"

"I'm very happy," she said as she brushed her tears away. "I've been waiting a hell of a long time for you to say that."

They both laughed, and Michael took her hand and led her toward the bedroom. They sat on the bed for a few minutes, and then he reached over and started to unbutton her blouse. She was filled with such desire for him. Her eyes glowed as he drew her to him.

"I love you, baby." His voice was heavy with emotion.

"Michael!" was all she was able to utter.

Moments later, they lay naked in the moonlight. He gently stroked her face, neck, and arms, and his hands moved down her body to her lovely white breasts. He kissed those creamy wonders, and her nipples became erect with excitement as his tongue skillfully sucked each one. His tongue moved down to her stomach, her belly, and then to her deliciously hot core, which was moist and waiting with anticipation.

Toni's hands gently glided through his soft, thick hair.

"Don't ever leave me," he pleaded, a feeling of vulnerability filling his deep-blue eyes.

"Never!" she said huskily. "Haven't you figured it out by now? I came back only for you."

As their passion ascended to higher plateaus, Michael softly licked her moist furnace, which swept waves of desire through her body. She whimpered under his touch and begged for him to enter her.

He relished every touch, every embrace, but finally he could stand it no longer. He climbed on top of her and plunged his manliness deep inside her. She let out a scream of delight, which quickly turned to soft, little moans as his thick bulk thrust deeper inside her to explore every sweet, loving recess of her core.

They floated deeper and deeper into their own private world, with Michael leading and Toni following. She screamed with delight, filling the quiet room with her love responses. Michael probed her every mystery as she opened herself wider for his exploration.

When they reached the final peak of their lovemaking, they exploded in a fury of ecstasy and slowly floated down into afterglow.

As they lay there quietly together, their limbs entwined, Toni found the peace she had lost so long ago.

Suddenly, she was overwhelmed with a feeling of sadness. It was as if all those long, lonely years away from him came back to haunt her. Tears filled her eyes and cascaded down her face. She sobbed like a baby, wracked with emotion.

"Honey, please don't cry," Michael consoled her. "It's all over now. We'll never be separated again." He kissed her eyes and face and whispered over and over again his love for her. Finally, after some time, Toni was able to get a hold of herself.

"Do you feel better now?" he asked gently.

She nodded a response. "I guess it was built up inside me for such a long time, and it just had to come out."

"Oh, baby." He held her close to him and caressed her hair with his hands.

"I never stopped loving you," Toni whispered. "I never could! You are my life. A part of me stopped living when I left you that day. I couldn't ever live without you again."

"You'll never have to," he assured her as he pulled her close to him and planted a kiss on her lips.

Michael sat up and looked for his clothes. He put his shirt and pants on and said he'd be back in a minute.

"Where are you going?" Toni asked.

He reached out to gently touch her face and said he'd be back shortly. A few minutes later, she heard the front door close and his footsteps coming toward the bedroom. He reached out his hand and gave her a tiny box.

"This is for you," he said, motioning for her to open it. "I've been holding it for a while. I hoped that one day I'd be able to give it to you again."

Toni took the box from Michael and opened it. There sat the emerald ring he had given her that summer day many years ago.

"Michael," she gasped, "I thought you gave this to Terri."

He shook his head. "This was my mom's ring. She gave it to me when we were in high school. She told me it was for that special person in my life. You're the only person that has ever been special to me."

Toni put her arms around him and kissed him softly. Michael took the ring from the box and put it on her finger.

"Now," he said, pretending to be bossy, "this is the last time I'm going to ask you." His voice changed to a gentle tone as he asked, "Will you marry me?"

"Yes," she whispered, and then teased him, "Did you really think you'd have to ask me more than once?"

Michael pulled Toni to him and fondled her hair. "Oh baby, baby!" was all he managed to get out.

The following morning, as daylight streamed through the window covering the lovers' faces, they woke to Michael's wonderfully hard manliness and spent the morning lost in the rapture of their lovemaking.

They decided to marry as soon as possible, and Michael called his mom and asked if they could stop by after breakfast. Toni did likewise, arranging to see her parents that afternoon.

When they entered Michael's parents' house, Madeline came running to them and hugged them both. Her eyes were filled with tears of happiness.

"Oh, Toni, I can't believe it. You and Michael at last."

"Yeah, Mom, we're pretty happy about it." Michael glowed and walked over to shake his father's hand, who was obviously moved by the good news.

"Hello, Mr. Jameson," Toni said. He always had a soft spot in his heart for her.

"Hello, Toni. My dear, you have made me a very happy man."

Toni laughed and said, "You'll just have an addition to the family."

"If I had to pick someone for Michael, it would be you." He smiled and squeezed her hand.

Michael was very moved by his father's words. Maybe he was starting to mellow in his old age.

Michael's parents asked where they would be spending their

honeymoon. The couple admitted they hadn't even thought about it. They volunteered their cabin, and Michael and Toni eagerly accepted.

After leaving Michael's parents, they went to the Lavini home. Helen Lavini cried when she heard the good news. She was a little disappointed that they weren't having a church wedding, but the couple expressed a wish to marry as soon as possible, and Helen understood. Mr. Lavini hugged his daughter, his eyes moist with tears.

"Well, my darling child, you are finally going to marry."

Toni smiled at her dad. He was the best dad a girl could wish for. She knew she was indeed fortunate to have such a loving father. "Dad," she gulped her words, "I'm very happy."

"I can see that," he responded, putting his arms around her shoulder and hugging her.

A civil ceremony was planned for the following Friday, with brunch to follow. The group consisted of the couple's families and Jason and Tracy, who would be their best man and matron of honor. They readily accepted when Michael and Toni called to give them the good news.

"We *knew* something was going on when you guys left the other night," Tracy teased. "We're very happy for you. It should have happened four years ago."

"Yes, it should have," Michael agreed. "But we're not going to look back, only ahead."

The week was filled with planning the wedding, arranging for the marriage license, and a thousand other minor details. As usual, when there is much to do, time flies, and Friday was soon upon them.

Toni woke much earlier than was necessary but really couldn't sleep. She had waited much too long for this day to waste it on unnecessary sleep. She lay in bed and thought of the past few months. For a moment, she thought of Noel. Sweet, loving Noel! She hoped he met someone and was as happy with that person as she was with Michael.

Michael returned to his apartment the night before. Although they had spent the week together at Toni's apartment, where they intended to live after the wedding, Toni didn't want him to see her in her dress until the wedding. She hustled him out, much to his dismay. He really couldn't figure out why women made such a fuss about weddings, but he agreed to do what she wished.

Toni looked at her dress hanging on the door. It was very pretty. Her mother had helped her pick it out, and she felt it was just right for her. She wanted to design her own dress, but owing to the time, she realized it would be impossible. She was satisfied with the one she chose. It was made of off-white taffeta with lace covering the collar and cuffs. The bodice was V-neck and also covered in lace, suggesting a slight hint of cleavage. Michael loved her breasts, and she didn't want to disappoint him on their wedding day. The skirt was A-line, falling just below the knees with shirring at the waist.

She finally dragged herself out of bed and went to run her bathwater. She planned on soaking for as long as she could until she had to get dressed. Her mother wasn't expected until 8:00 a.m., and it was only six thirty, so she planned on relaxing in the tub and letting her thoughts float away.

This was the happiest day of her life! This is what she had hoped and prayed for many years, and now her dreams were becoming a reality. She remembered Michael's face as he kissed her good night the evening before. His eyes were full of love for her.

"I never thought this would happen, but we've been given a second chance, and I plan to make you the happiest woman in the world."

After an hour of soaking, Toni reluctantly got out. She decided to put on her undergarments and robe and to wait for her mother's arrival. Helen Lavini told her daughter she wanted to help her dress, but Toni sensed she was really coming just to be with her for a while before the wedding.

Toni made herself a cup of coffee and opened the paper. A few minutes later, the doorbell rang. She thought her mom had probably decided to come early and went to answer the intercom.

"Good morning, the future Mrs. Jameson," he said playfully.

"Michael!" she gasped with alarm. "What are you doing here?"

"I wanted to get a peek at the bride."

"I have no intention of letting you see me until we get to City Hall."

"I know, honey," he responded softly. "I just came to tell you for the hundredth time how much I love you."

Toni smiled and said, "I love you too."

"See you soon, honey," he said, and he was gone.

Toni realized how fortunate she was to have such a wonderful man as Michael. The past week had gone by as if she were in a dream. To sleep with Michael every night was something she would never become accustomed to.

A few minutes later, Helen arrived and helped her daughter dress. With every passing minute, Toni was becoming more nervous.

"Honey, try to calm down," she urged.

"Yeah sure, Mom," Toni said impatiently. "It's not every day you get married."

"It'll be over before you know it," she said sweetly.

"No, Mom. It'll never be over. It's going to last a lifetime."

Luckily, the hour passed very quickly as Toni's mother recalled memories of her as a child. Toni's father and brother arrived shortly after to drive them to the courthouse.

"Well, sis, you two finally did it," Tim said, as he gave Toni a hug. "I wish you every happiness." She hugged her brother back.

"Come on. We should be going," Mr. Lavini said, and they readied themselves to leave.

Michael and his parents were seated in the waiting room. They were there for a while before Toni and her family arrived.

"Michael, I want you to know how pleased we are that you're marrying Toni." Michael gave a start. He hadn't expected his father to be so direct. It just wasn't like him. "Your mom and I wish you all the happiness in the world."

For the second time in a few days, Michael felt moved by his father's words. He thanked him and fell into silence.

His father never seemed to be satisfied with him when he was growing up and constantly expressed his discontentment, but after Michael married Terri, he seemed to mellow. He sensed his mother had something to do with this transformation. To

Michael, his mother was the greatest lady in the world—aside from Toni, of course. He loved her very much. She was always very supportive of any decision he made, as long as she felt he had really thought it through. She was the exact opposite of his father.

When Michael left Toni the night before, he went to see his parents. His father had already gone to bed, but his mother was still up.

"Honey, what a surprise," Madeline said pleasantly. "Prewedding jitters?"

"No, Mom. I just wanted to see you and tell you how much I love you."

"I love you too, honey, and I know you'll be happy." Madeline Jameson got up from where she was seated, came over to her son, and put her arms around him. She loved him very much and always felt sad that he and John never got along. From the time Michael was small, John never seemed happy with the boy. She could never understand why. She tried to talk to her husband about Michael, but he would either clam up or leave the house in a rage. Michael was such a bright little boy, and Madeline spent years of her life defending him to John. He was always so hard on Michael and made him feel so inadequate, especially when Michael decided to go into construction rather than going to college.

She went on, "I love you too, honey, and I know you and Toni will be very happy. Your father agrees. She's the kind of girl I've always wanted for you." Michael seemed to tense up for a moment, and she thought he would say something about John, but he didn't.

"I never thought I could love anyone the way I love Toni."

"I know, honey." His mother squeezed his hand.

"Well, I guess I'll go. Tomorrow's a big day!"

Madeline smiled as she watched him walk to his car. She wanted for him whatever it was he wanted. She hoped that Toni would help him find himself.

Michael looked up when he heard Toni's family enter the waiting room. He looked for Toni but didn't see her. Helen Lavini noticed the apprehension on his face and said calmly, "Don't worry, Michael. She's coming. We met Jason and Tracy in the hallway. She'll be in soon."

A moment later, Michael saw her enter the room. He stood up and walked over to her, unable to remember ever seeing her look as beautiful as she did this morning. When she saw him, she smiled and reached for his hand.

"Well, shall we begin?" the attendant said and led them into the judge's quarters.

"Dearly beloved ..." Toni looked at Michael as the judge began speaking. She couldn't recall ever seeing him look so handsome. He was dressed in a dark-blue suit with a light-blue shirt and a carnation in his lapel matching the color of his shirt. The carnation also matched the bouquet Toni's mother had selected for her. The shirt brought out the blue in his eyes, and she saw that he had such a sense of peace on his face, the same peace that she was feeling in her heart.

"Do you, Antoinette, take this man to be your lawful, wedded husband, to have and to hold, in sickness and in health, from this day forward?"

"I do," Toni said, as she looked at Michael tenderly.

"And do you, Michael, take this woman to be your lawful,

wedded wife, to have and to hold, in sickness and in health, from this day forward?"

"I do."

"The rings, please." Jason stepped forward to hand the judge the rings, and a moment later, they were man and wife. Michael leaned over to kiss his darling Toni. His lips felt as if a rose petal was brushing across them.

Everyone surrounded them to congratulate them. Some were crying, but they all were as happy as the loving couple.

Toni felt as if she had just been through a dream. Everything happened so quickly, and Michael, her Michael, was standing by her side, holding her hand. His hand was so warm, as warm as his loving heart.

The group left for the restaurant together. Michael and Toni walked a little behind them. He squeezed her hand and asked, "How do you feel?"

"I think I'm in shock, to tell you the truth."

"Me too," he agreed, "but it's the happiest feeling I've ever experienced."

Toni looked into his eyes and thought for a moment he was going to cry. For what seemed like a lifetime, they held their gaze until finally a voice brought them back to the present.

"Hey, you guys," Tim yelled, "are you going to come to eat or stand there looking at each other all day?" They laughed and hurried on.

The wedding breakfast turned out to be a delightful affair, and by noon, the couple was on their way to the Jameson cabin. Michael had borrowed his father's car for the week, knowing that Toni wasn't fond of the bucket seats in the Mustang.

"Come over here, honey," he coaxed.

She moved over next to him and rested her head on his shoulder. The day had been wonderful but exhausting. She still had to pinch herself to believe it was real. For so many years, she had wanted this, and now it had come true.

CHAPTER 11

*I*t seemed as if they spent much more than two hours on the road, but finally Michael turned off onto the country road that would take them to his parents' cabin. The cabin was nestled in the woods by a picturesque little pond, surrounded by pine and spruce trees. Michael and Toni had spent many happy moments there, and it seemed right that they should return there to celebrate their marriage.

Michael turned the key in the lock and lifted Toni to carry her across the threshold. She laughed at that and commented on how old-fashioned he was.

"I'm just a sentimental guy, honey," he replied tenderly.

The cabin was perfect in every way. It appeared as if it had just been tidied up, and the fire was blazing away. On the table, the couple found a bottle of champagne on ice and a note:

> Our darling children,
> Mrs. Jones came by to make sure everything was

fine for your arrival. We wanted it to be perfect.
Many years of happiness.

Love,

Mom and Dad

Toni was very touched by the Jamesons' efforts to make the cabin as comfortable as possible for them. Michael had mixed feelings and said his mother probably planned everything. He then went on to relay the conversation with his father earlier in the day. Toni commented on how his father seemed to be changing.

"He loves you, honey," Michael commented. "You know how to soften him up. That's why he was so pleased today."

"That's not why, Michael. He loves you too, even though he's not able to communicate that to you."

Michael dropped the subject. He didn't particularly want to get into an argument over his father on their honeymoon.

They sat by the fire, hypnotized by the flames as the wood crackled and broke up. Life had become so good! Michael opened the bottle of champagne, and they spent the rest of the afternoon holding each other and watching the fire die.

"Honey, are you hungry?" Michael asked.

"Only for you," she whispered.

He took her face in his hands and lost himself in her eyes. Again, for a moment, she thought he was close to tears, but he managed to stop them from coming.

"Come on, darling," he said, and Toni followed him into the bedroom.

"I missed you last night," he said as he started to undress. "I had a hard time sleeping without you."

"I missed you too, but it was well worth waiting for."

"Did I tell you how beautiful you looked today?"

"Did I tell you I can't remember when you looked more handsome?"

He came over to her, picked her up, and gently laid her on the bed.

A worried look crossed Toni's face. "It won't change, will it, Michael?"

"What?"

"What we're feeling. You're not going to get used to me, are you?"

"Never," he said, as he buried his hands in her soft auburn hair.

Michael started to kiss her everywhere as he undressed her slowly. Toni's hands found the buckle on his belt and started to undo it. She found her way to his zipper and started working his pants off.

Soon they were completely nude, and Michael pulled Toni to him and said huskily, "You are so beautiful," holding his breath as his eyes took in every part of her body.

Moments later, they were wrapped in each other's arms, and Michael's hands slowly moved up and down Toni's body, wanting to feel every part of her. Her hands moved down to his throbbing bulk. As she stroked it slowly and deliberately, it began to respond to her touch. Soon, they were lost in their own private world again, but this time every kiss, every caress was deep and tender. Michael kissed her gently, wanting the night to last forever.

"Oh, my darling," Toni whispered as he awoke strong feelings of desire in her. His lips kissed her mouth, ears, and neck and moved down to her wondrous white peaks. He playfully ran his tongue over each nipple, making them stand hard from his kisses. His mouth found the crevice between her breasts and he ran his tongue up and down, pausing for a moment before returning to those delicious wonders.

A tingling sensation was building in the innermost part of Toni, growing with each kiss. When Michael had filled himself with her snow-white breasts, he moved his tongue down over her tummy to her wonderfully hot mystery, which awaited him with growing excitement. Moments later, Michael found this dark, luscious place and moaned loudly as his largeness slipped into her hot liquid nest. Toni screamed with delight at his initial thrust. Then he lay quietly inside her for a moment until his manliness started to move slowly and deliberately in and out of her.

Toni couldn't contain herself anymore. She lifted her legs to meet his every thrust, allowing him to enter her deeper. Animal moans came from her throat, directing him which ways to move to please her the most. That sweet, dark forest was a mystery he wanted to explore for an eternity. His favorite place was deep inside her, delighting in the things he felt and the feelings she gave to him.

Minutes turned into hours and hours into days. Their love-making took on heightened ecstasy as the time went by, bringing them closer together spiritually as well as physically.

Toni never knew she could feel such fulfillment. All the feelings they felt for each other in high school came back that week to strengthen a bond that could never again be broken.

The night before they were to return to St. Paul, Michael said sadly, "We have to go home tomorrow, honey."

"I know." She sighed softly. "I wish we could stay forever. We've been so happy here."

"And we'll be happy in our apartment also," Michael concluded.

They spoke for a while longer, and Toni mentioned the idea of Michael returning to school. He tensed up at the suggestion, and she didn't pursue it.

The lovers fell asleep in each other's arms as an owl cooed in the distance.

CHAPTER 12

*M*r. Shapiro was happy to see Toni back at work on the following Monday, and she was eager to begin again, to keep her mind off the past evening.

The couple returned to St. Paul the afternoon before, and Michael went to his apartment to collect some of his things. He had a few weeks to clear out the apartment and decided to do it gradually, not causing too much of an inconvenience for him. When he returned, he seemed somewhat distant. Toni didn't think much of it because she felt there may have been lots of memories in his apartment causing the reaction, or it was finally starting to sink in that he was really married to her, which would alone be enough to cause him to retreat into a world of his own.

Later that evening, after they had finished dinner, he still seemed preoccupied.

"Michael, is there anything bothering you?" Toni asked, a worried tone to her voice.

"No," he replied curtly.

Toni let it go and busied herself with unpacking from their honeymoon. As bedtime approached, she changed her clothes and then went to Michael, who was reading in the living room.

"Will you be coming to bed soon?"

"No." His voice was a little too gruff for her not to be concerned.

"Michael, what's wrong?"

"Nothing, nothing." He waved her away uneasily.

"Why are you speaking to me that way?" Apprehension filled her face.

"Stop nagging me, will you?" he shouted, his face red with anger.

With that, she burst into tears and headed for the bedroom, hoping he would follow her and calm her fears. He didn't. He continued to sit, reading in the living room. She couldn't understand what could have caused the abrupt change in her loving husband. Maybe he didn't love her and just wanted to get back at her. She couldn't believe that. He loved her! She knew he did. Nobody could be that good an actor. Her head pounded with pain. She got up, went to the bathroom to take some aspirin, and then went back to bed. Finally, she was thrown into a deep sleep. She had no idea when he came to bed. She just wanted to block out the whole incident and hoped that things would be back to normal the following day.

The following morning, things weren't much better. Michael was very quiet. He got up before her, and she woke when she heard him in the shower. She feigned sleep as he came into the bedroom to dress for work. He dressed quickly, took his coat, and quietly closed the door so as not to wake her. She sobbed into her pillow as she heard the door close. She really didn't know how she would be able to make it through the day without someone at work detecting her mental state. She was hopeful that when Michael returned that evening, whatever was bothering him would be worked out.

Monday dragged on for Toni. Even though she had a lot of work to catch up on, she was tempted to call him. Fear forced its way into her heart, and she couldn't bring herself to do it. If his mood hadn't changed, she wasn't capable of dealing with him.

When the day came to an end, Toni hoped Michael would be waiting for her outside her building, but he wasn't, and she boarded the bus to take her home. She tried to concentrate on her newspaper, but tears started to stream down her face. She felt humiliated, riding on a public bus, thinking someone would notice. She managed to hold the paper in front of her face so that nobody would detect her tears. As she brushed the tears away, more fell to take their place. It was a futile battle. She finally gave up and let the tears fall onto her clothing.

When she arrived home, there was a note waiting for her.

> Toni,
> I went to my apartment. I'll be working there until late tonight. Don't wait up.
>
> Michael

She sat down, blew her nose, and then went to the bathroom to wash her face. She looked like a mess. The fear that had forced its way into her being slowly turned to dread. How long could this game he was playing go on? She was furious at him for treating her this way. She thought of calling his apartment but decided to just leave him alone. He would eventually have to work it out on his own.

Toni couldn't understand why Michael was closing himself off to her. The honeymoon was perfect in every way. They had grown so close together that week. Could something have happened to frighten him? She didn't know. As long as he refused to speak to her, she couldn't find out.

Toni poured herself into her work, spending the whole night sketching some new designs. She knew if she just sat around watching TV, she'd be a basket case. She had to be strong and hope for the best. At 11:00 p.m., she wearily fell into bed and was fast asleep when Michael's key turned in the door. He entered the bedroom, undressed quietly with the light off, and got into bed. He made no attempt to hold her in his arms but just rolled over and fell off to sleep.

After a week of this behavior, Toni couldn't stand it any longer. "Please talk to me," she pleaded with him.

"There's nothing to say," he responded dryly.

"All right," she decided, "if you don't want to talk to me, will you consider speaking with a professional?"

Michael looked at her intently and said, "I'm having some personal problems now. I'm sorry if they're affecting you, but there's nothing I can do about it."

"Yes, there is," Toni said firmly. "You can speak to someone who can help you. Are you willing to do that?"

"I need to be alone today. Can I give you the answer later?"

Toni agreed to that, and Michael put on his coat and left.

She didn't know where he was going. She supposed back to his old apartment. He still had many of his things there, so she assumed he was spending his time working.

A few days later, Michael told Toni he was willing to see someone. A friend at work gave her the name of a very reputable psychologist, and she made an appointment to see her the following afternoon.

"Hello," the tall, dark-haired lady greeted Toni brightly. "My name is Leslie Adams." She had a very warm quality, and Toni immediately felt at ease with her.

"How can I help you?" Toni smiled, for she felt that perhaps this lady could help Michael with his problems.

"I'm here really about my husband," she began. "He's having some problems, and Jane Andrews referred me to you."

"Your husband?" Her voice sounded so soothing. "What's the problem?"

Toni went on to relate how she had met Michael, their separation, and their recent courtship ending in marriage. She was describing their honeymoon and how happy they had been when it all became too much for her, and she burst into tears. She sat there sobbing for a while, embarrassed by her behavior in front of a complete stranger.

Leslie walked over to her with a tissue box in her hand. "It's all right," she said calmly. Toni wiped her eyes, blew her nose, and thanked her, trying hard to force a smile.

"You love your husband very much, don't you?" She looked up to see a pair of kind blue eyes staring at her.

"Yes," she replied weakly.

"What do you think is the reason for Michael's sudden change in behavior?"

"I don't know. Well, there is one thing. It's silly, but you might want to know about it. I left Michael to go to school four years ago. I wanted him to come with me, but he wouldn't go. I never saw him so angry when I asked him. He insisted on staying here. I thought he blamed me all these years for our breakup, but when he asked me to marry him, I felt that it was in the past."

Leslie walked to her desk and leaned against it, facing Toni. "I'm going to make an appointment to see Michael. He has agreed to come here, hasn't he?"

"Yes," Toni replied, trying to allay her fears.

"My advice to you, and I intend to tell Michael the same thing, is to try and act civil toward one another. So many times when couples are having problems, they create more tension by alienating each other; sleeping in separate beds, eating alone, and so forth. Don't do that. It will only put more of a strain on the relationship." She paused for a moment and then went on.

"Do you have anything to keep yourself occupied during this difficult period?"

"Yes," Toni responded. "I have my work. We're very busy now. I could stay overtime."

"It's better if you work at home instead. Michael is going to need your support now. From what you tell me, it sounds like he's going through a tough time." Toni confirmed that, and Leslie continued.

"Keep in touch with your friends and family. Don't isolate yourself. That will only make it harder on you. I don't know how long it will take to get to the source of Michael's problem. It depends on how honest he is with himself and how much he wants to change. This will all be hard on you, Toni. I know that, but try to be strong."

"I love him with all my heart."

Leslie nodded. "That is to his advantage."

Toni left Leslie's office feeling a lot better. As long as Michael was willing to see her, she was confident that, in time, whatever was bothering him would be worked out.

For the second time in three months, she felt that there was a ray of hope.

CHAPTER 13

"Hello, Michael," Leslie greeted him, with a big smile on her face. "I'm Leslie Adams." He seemed nervous and moved uncomfortably in his chair. "I met your wife the other day," she added. "She seems very nice." For a moment, she thought she saw a reaction in his eyes, but he said nothing to indicate a response. Leslie could see that what was bothering him would be hard to get at.

"Do you want to talk?"

"That's what I'm here for, isn't it?" he said dryly.

Leslie smiled and said, "I understand you were just married. Your second marriage, right?"

"Yes," he responded, his eyes moving around the room as if he were a bored child in a doctor's office.

"What was your first wife like?"

"She wasn't Toni," he declared emphatically.

"Oh?" Leslie said. "How were they different?"

"Toni is smart."

"Oh, I see," Leslie responded. "Do you feel she's smarter than you?"

"No, not necessarily, but if she sees something she wants, she goes right after it. She's always been very ambitious."

"Do you admire her for that?"

Leslie's question surprised Michael. "Well, sure! She went to school to become a designer, and now she has a great future."

"And you, Michael? What do you want to do?"

"I'm in construction," he responded quickly.

"No, what do you *want* to do? Toni mentioned to me that you were interested in architecture."

Michael fidgeted in his chair and fixed his eyes on an object in the room. He wouldn't look at Leslie, though. She sensed she had touched a nerve, made a note of it, and decided to pursue it later.

"How is your marriage going?"

"You know how it's going. That's why I'm here," he said.

"Do you have any idea why your behavior changed toward Toni?"

"No, I just feel pressured. I mean, the honeymoon was great, but when we got back, I realized that we were *really* married and started to feel closed in."

"Did you have this kind of reaction to your marriage to Terri?"

"No. I didn't love Terri. She loved me, and I thought I could make our marriage work. I found out the hard way that one-sided love affairs are bound to fail."

Leslie again made a note of Michael's response and discussed with him what she had with Toni a few days earlier. She stressed how important it was for them to continue living together as man and wife. Michael agreed to try.

"How long is this going to take?" he asked uneasily.

"What do you mean?"

"Well, how long will I have to see you?"

"That depends on you, Michael, and how willing you are to deal with your problems."

Michael fell silent and looked away.

When he returned home that evening, the apartment was dark except for a light coming from Toni's workroom. He opened the door and found her asleep at her drawing table. He smiled when he saw her and said, "Come on, honey. Let's go to bed."

"Michael?" she said, half asleep, astonished by his tenderness.

He lifted her into his arms and carried her into the bedroom, where he gently deposited her on the bed. He went to take a shower, and when he returned, she was fast asleep. He undressed her and pulled the covers up over her. Then he looked down at her, and tears suddenly sprang to his eyes.

"Oh, God! Why am I doing this?" he asked himself. "Please help me."

He undressed and slipped in next to Toni, took her in his arms, and whispered, "I love you, Toni." Then he fell off to sleep.

The following day, when Toni arrived at work, she decided to call Tracy and see if she was free for lunch. She needed some close female companionship and felt she couldn't tell her mother what was bothering her. They arranged to meet at Mickey's Diner, an old coffee shop in downtown St. Paul. When Toni walked into the restaurant, Tracy had already arrived. She took one look at Toni and said in an alarmed tone, "Good God, girl! What has happened to you?" She looked very tired with rings under her eyes.

"I've been working long hours, and I think it's catching up with me."

"Honey, don't try to bullshit me. I've known you too long for that."

"Oh, Tracy," she sighed, "don't tell Jason, please."

"Honey, don't worry. This is girl talk."

Toni told her what she had been through since the return from their honeymoon. Tracy's face filled with concern.

"Oh, honey," she said, "give him some time. He loves you very much. He hurt real bad when you left for school. He disappeared for two weeks, and nobody knew where he went."

Surprised by this story, Toni asked, "Where did he go?"

"We don't know to this day. You know that he holds his feelings inside. I personally don't think it's a healthy way to live, but we women are all mouth, and men are closed mouths."

Toni agreed with her observation. "He started to see a therapist."

"Michael?" Tracy was astounded by the news. "Good for him."

"She's very warm and supportive. If anyone can find out what's bothering him, she can."

"Everything will be all right. You know, this is just as hard on you as it is on Michael. I mean, for him to withdraw from you like that. What advice did she give you?"

"She told me to stay busy," Toni responded. "I intend to see a lot of you and my family during this period."

"Fine with me, honey," Tracy said cheerfully.

As they left the restaurant together, Toni realized that what Tracy said was true. Everything would be all right, and she had to lay her fears aside. Tracy kissed her, and they promised to see one another soon. Then Toni headed back to work. She decided that an optimistic attitude would be her best approach. Moping around wasn't going to help herself or Michael.

When she arrived home that evening, she found Michael setting the table for dinner. He had already warmed up the meal she had prepared the evening before.

"Hi!" he greeted her cheerfully as she came in the door.

"Hi," she responded quietly.

"I thought I'd cook tonight. You don't mind, do you?"

"Not at all," she replied, relieved to be able to relax for a while.

"I got used to cooking when I lived by myself," Michael interjected.

Toni smiled and sat down on the couch, admiring him in her apron. Suddenly she realized how tired she was and decided not to work that evening and just relax for a change.

"How was your day?" Michael asked brightly.

"Okay. Busy as usual."

"I guess you know I saw Leslie Adams yesterday."

"Yes, I know." She refrained from asking him how it went, feeling that it would be better if he volunteered the information.

"She's very nice," Michael observed.

"I thought so too."

Michael came over and sat next to her on the couch. "Toni, I feel like a heel, I mean the way I've been treating you."

Toni looked at him, surprised by his honesty. He seemed torn between his feelings for her and what was eating away at him. She reached for his hand and held it. He made no attempt to pull it away.

"You're having a hard time right now. I'm sure you'll work it out."

"I'm sorry I hurt you," he said. "I didn't mean to."

"I know, Michael."

They spent the rest of the evening watching an old movie on TV. Michael and Toni were civil to each other, but he made no overture toward her, and she felt it was better that it came from him.

After the movie, they went to bed and fell asleep in each other's arms. Toni wondered how long she could last without making love to him.

On the second visit to Leslie, Michael felt more at ease. She had a way about her that made him feel comfortable. Michael decided he had to solve his problem and would be as honest as was necessary to do so.

"Hello, Michael." She smiled brightly as he came into the office. "Well, you seem a little happier than the last time I saw you."

"I am," he admitted. "I've decided to make a commitment to solving this problem. Since this happened, I don't like myself very much, especially the way I've treated Toni."

"I'm glad to hear that you want to work on this."

"Where do I begin?" he asked uneasily.

"How are things at home?"

"Okay. I mean, as well as can be expected."

"How is Toni?" Leslie asked softly.

"She's okay. She's a real trooper."

"It has to have taken its toll on her."

"I know," he agreed, "but she's trying hard to be as optimistic as possible."

"Is there anything that happened on your honeymoon to create such a change in you?"

Michael thought for a while about the question but answered, "No."

"This isn't going to be easy," Leslie commented. "I think you know that. We may have to look deep into your past to find out what's bothering you. I'm not altogether convinced that Toni is the cause but rather the symptom."

Michael looked down for a moment, moved uncomfortably in his chair, and after a few moments of silence, said adamantly, "Ask whatever you want. I love Toni, and I'll be damned if I'm going to lose her again."

Leslie nodded. "How did you two meet?"

"It's a long story."

"That's what I'm here for—to listen."

"We met during our senior year of high school. I had a steady, but things had been pretty stale between us for a long time."

"What was her name?" she asked.

"Terri, my first wife."

Leslie made a note of that and continued to question him. "How long did you and Toni date?"

"We went together during our senior year. In fact, we broke up a few weeks before graduation."

"What was your relationship like?"

"Right from the start, I felt at peace with her."

"Can you be more specific?" Leslie asked. "You know, try to give me some details."

Michael nodded and went on. "I immediately felt comfortable with her. It was like I could talk to her about anything."

Leslie nodded and indicated he should continue.

"On our first date, I wanted to ask her to go steady. I remember that we went to the falls, and I felt so close to her. I wanted to ask her that evening but couldn't."

"Why didn't you ask her?"

"I was still going with Terri," he explained.

Leslie looked surprised at that and said, "Why were you still going with Terri if you were dating Toni?"

Michael became uncomfortable and began to fidget in his chair.

"Would you like to come back to that, Michael?"

He seemed surprised at the question and nodded.

"My job is to make you feel comfortable too. If you're not ready to speak about something, tell me, and we'll move on." He was apparently relieved by that bit of information.

"So, you and Toni spent your senior year together. What kind of things did you do?"

"I guess the kind of things that people in love do. We spent lots of time together—talking, going to movies, driving to my parents' cabin, making love."

Leslie raised her eyebrows at that. "You had a sexual relationship during that year?" He nodded. "How did you manage that? You both lived at home, didn't you?"

"Yeah, but my parents used to go away some weekends, and Toni's parents went out every Saturday night. Her younger brother never seemed to be around, so it was easy for me to slip into her bedroom. She had an entrance off the front porch."

"Were there other high school students your age making love?"

"I think that the steadies were. I don't think they talked about it, though. I'm pretty sure my best friend, Jason, was but even he didn't say anything."

"What was your sex life like?"

Michael appeared very flustered. "Man, do we have to talk about this? You're a woman!" he exclaimed.

"I'm your therapist first, Michael. A woman second." He seemed to calm down a little at that, but she sensed it was still hard for him to talk about his sex life.

"Michael," Leslie indicated for him to continue.

"Our sex life was the best. Really great! Toni was pretty inexperienced, but she was eager to learn."

"Where did your experience come from?"

"When I was with Terri, we had sex a lot."

"How long did you go with her?"

"Two years," he replied.

Leslie made a note of that. "You mentioned before that you didn't love Terri. Why, then, did you have a sexual relationship with her?"

"She loved me and said she wanted me. I was never one to deny a woman what she wanted."

"Oh," Leslie replied. "So, it had nothing to do with your sexual urges?"

"Well, yes, I guess it did. I like sex; I always have. I mean it makes me feel real good."

"How old were you when you had your first sexual experience?"

"God, Leslie!" Michael exclaimed, disconcerted by her questions.

"I know this is hard, Michael, but I have to get to know you, and the only way I can is by you telling me these things." She continued, "Why don't you think about this for next time." Michael nodded.

When Michael left Leslie's office, he felt utterly drained. He realized that this was going to be a lot harder than he anticipated.

Hi, Michael." Toni smiled warmly as he walked in the door.

"Hi," he said quietly and fell into the recliner.

"You look beat," Toni observed.

"Yeah, I am. I never thought therapy would be so hard."

Toni busied herself preparing dinner. She was aware that Michael seemed more willing to talk to her about the sessions.

"She asked me all kinds of questions about sex."

"Really?" Toni replied. "I guess she wants to get an idea of how you feel about certain things."

Michael went on. "She asked about us, how we met, you know that stuff and Terri."

Toni didn't respond much to that. She felt on some level that what went on with Leslie was his business, but he pressed on, having a need to talk to her.

"She's a really nice woman and seems to know what she's doing."

"I'm happy for you," Toni commented.

After dinner, they sat on the couch and talked.

"There's something I've wanted to talk with you about."

"What is it?" he asked.

"It's been two weeks since we returned from our honeymoon. I know you've been going through a lot, but have you thought at all when we will begin making love again?"

"I've thought about it a lot," he said, his voice full of concern. "I think about it all the time, but I don't feel I'm ready yet."

"Do you have any suggestions for what I should do in the meantime?" she asked quietly, not wishing for a confrontation with him.

Michael looked at her. He could imagine how miserable she was feeling and suddenly felt ill at ease. "I don't know," he stammered.

Toni put her hand in his and said softly, "Can you at least hold me if you can't make love to me right now? You've opened up all kinds of feelings in me, and now I'm left hanging."

He became irritated by that and snapped, "Well, maybe you should get a lover to tide you over for the duration."

"Oh, sure!" Toni screamed, unable to contain her rage. "What is that going to solve but drive us further apart from each other?" Her anger turned to tears, and she ran into the bedroom and slammed the door.

Michael wanted to kick himself for that. Hadn't he hurt her enough? It seemed lately that was all he was doing. Maybe their marriage was all a bad mistake. He felt like he wanted to explode. Instead, he reached for his coat and walked back to the bedroom door. He knocked lightly and told Toni he was going out for a while, but she didn't respond.

The following morning at breakfast Toni suggested quietly, "Will you ask Leslie if she has any ideas?"

"Yes, I will." He reached over and kissed her lightly on the lips. She pulled back a little, frightened of her vulnerability.

The days seemed to go by slowly. Funny, Toni thought, how fast they passed when she and Michael had been happy. Three months had gone by since Michael started therapy. He seemed to be high-strung most of the time and would constantly say things to hurt her without thinking and then apologize later for his behavior. Toni realized she was fortunate to have the patience of a saint. Any other person would have been out the door long before this.

She wondered if therapy was really helping him. He never volunteered what happened in the sessions anymore, appearing self-involved most of the time.

Mr. Shapiro couldn't help but notice the change in Toni's attitude. She had always had an abundance of energy, but now it seemed she had become a driven personality. The quality of her work was still excellent, but she threw herself into it and never seemed to come up for air. Much of her optimistic spirit seemed to be drained from her. One day, he came to her and asked her out to lunch. She happily accepted. They planned to go out that very day to the Hilton.

When they settled in at their table, Mr. Shapiro asked hesitantly, "Well, Toni, are you still enjoying your honeymoon?"

She seemed uncomfortable with the question but answered, "Yes, it's fine," aware that she wasn't convincing him for one minute. She added, "Mr. Shapiro, is there something wrong with my work?"

"Oh no, dear." He smiled at her. "But there's obviously something wrong with you."

"I really can't talk about it." She sighed and looked away.

"I wish you would, Toni. I want you to know you can come to me with your problems, if you wish."

Toni felt touched by her employer's kindness. "Thank you for the offer." She forced a smile. "Michael and I are having some difficulties, but I'm sure we'll work them out."

Mr. Shapiro sensed what she was saying was true, and he was glad she felt comfortable enough around him to tell him so.

"Toni, my reason for asking you to lunch is twofold. Not just to inquire about your family, but also to make you an interesting offer."

"What is it, Mr. Shapiro?" she asked, her curiosity growing.

"I'm thinking of sending you to New York. From what I see, you could use a vacation. In a few weeks, the Coliseum will be holding the National Designers' show. I'd like you to attend as a representative for our firm. Would you like to go?"

Toni smiled broadly and said, "That's just what the doctor ordered." She wanted to kiss her boss for suggesting it. To get away from St. Paul for a while was exactly what she needed. She loved the idea of returning to New York. Perhaps she could go by F.I.T. and visit her favorite instructors.

"Then it's settled," her boss commented brightly.

"When will I be leaving, and how long will I be staying?"

"In a week or so, and you can stay as long as you want, up to a week."

"Sounds good to me," Toni commented.

CHAPTER 14

*M*ichael walked into Leslie's office and hoped that this time he wouldn't end up feeling so shaken. The last session had really thrown him.

Leslie greeted him and motioned for him to sit down.

"How was your week?" she asked pleasantly. From the look on his face, things weren't going too well.

"One day is good, the other bad. I find myself screaming at Toni for no reason at all. I feel like a jerk most of the time."

"Are you feeling a lot of pressure?"

"Yeah. Most of the time, I feel uptight. My friends at work say I'm a real grouch."

"That's a pretty natural reaction to therapy, Michael. It's very hard to talk about all these things."

"You can say that again!" he blurted out. "I never thought it'd be like this."

"Last week was really hard, wasn't it?" Leslie asked softly. He nodded in agreement.

"Tell me if you begin to feel uncomfortable. If you don't

want to talk about something, we can always come back to it later."

"Yeah, but we have to deal with it eventually, right? It might as well be now."

"All right, if that's what you wish." Leslie paused for a moment and then said, "What were we talking about last week?"

"You asked me when I had my first sexual experience."

"Yes, that's right," she recalled.

"Well," Michael began, "I think I was about eight or so. There was a girl on my block. What was her name?" He searched his mind to remember. "I can't recall, but anyway, we used to play doctor." Michael laughed nervously. He still had a hard time relating his intimate sexual behavior to a woman.

"What was it like for you, Michael?"

"I don't know." Again, a nervous laugh. "I always had a lot of fun."

"Sex makes you feel good, then?"

"Doesn't it for everyone?" he responded matter-of-factly. "I think that's the one area in life where I feel accepted."

Leslie made a note of that comment and continued. "You mean you didn't feel accepted by your parents?"

"My mom, yes," he said emphatically. "My dad ..." His voice trailed off, and then he grew silent. After a minute, he began again. "My dad and I never got along." He smiled weakly, trying to cover up his nervousness. "He's a real hard guy."

"How was he hard on you?" she probed gently.

Michael flinched, his discomfort tremendously apparent. Suddenly his tone was full of rage, his face red with anger. "He never made me feel like he cared for me. I could never do anything right in his eyes."

"Can you give me an example?"

"An example?" He laughed a humorless laugh. "How about my whole life?"

When he calmed down, he felt completely drained and asked, "Do we have to talk about this now?"

"No, Michael," Leslie assured him, "we don't have to. But we'll have to talk about it sooner or later, right?"

A horrible feeling of dread forced its way into his heart. He abruptly changed the subject to Toni and their problem. He asked Leslie for suggestions, and she told him it would be best if Toni came to the next session with him. He told her he'd speak with Toni about it.

When Michael returned home that evening, Toni wasn't there. He sensed her absence as if a hole were in his heart. He was suddenly overwhelmed with a need to see her and hold her, to tell her how much she meant to him. He knew she was feeling very alone, and he wanted to ease her pain. He also needed to ease his own. He decided to go pick her up at work.

When Toni came out of her building, the Mustang was parked at the curb. A rush of joy filled her heart. This was the first overture Michael had made toward her in some time.

When she got into the car, he smiled and leaned over to kiss her. Her heart beat rapidly. It was filled with love for him, and she honestly didn't know how much longer she could go on without him. She needed him desperately, and to feel such deprivation was more than she could stand. At the same time, she needed to remove herself from the situation for her own self-preservation. She decided to tell Michael about her upcoming trip to New York that very evening.

"Would you like to eat out tonight?" he asked pleasantly.

"Sounds good to me." She smiled brightly at her husband. They decided on Chinese food and went to their favorite neighborhood restaurant.

After dinner, on their way home, Michael commented, "I spoke to Leslie as you asked me." Toni nodded. "She wants to see both of us the next time I go." He hesitated for a moment and then continued, "I know how you've been feeling. I'm feeling the same way. I don't know when I felt as alone as I did when I went home and you weren't there."

Toni looked at him as he spoke. Michael was always candid when he knew what he was feeling. She knew her timing was off, but felt she had to tell him about the trip.

"Mr. Shapiro asked me to represent the firm at the National Designers' Show in New York, and I accepted. I really need to get away for a little while, Michael."

He was stunned by the news and pulled the car over to the curb. "I don't understand," he said, his eyes full of apprehension. "Are you thinking of leaving me?"

Tears welled up in Toni's eyes as he said that. "You have such little faith in me, Michael?"

When he realized what he asked, he felt horrible. "Oh, honey, I'm sorry," he said, reaching out for her hand.

"These damn bucket seats!" Toni scoffed as she dried her tears. "Why is it that whenever we're going through a crisis, we're in this car?" They both laughed, and the tension cleared from the air.

"In answer to your question, no, I'm not leaving you. I'm taking a business trip." She paused for a moment and then continued. "I admire you very much, Michael. I know how painful what you're going through is, but that hasn't stopped you. You still keep going. It takes a lot of courage on your part." Michael was silent. "My boss asked me to go. I really can't turn him down. He has been so good to me. Also, I don't think it would hurt for us to be apart from each other for a while. You've been under such stress lately."

"How long will you be gone?" he asked hesitantly.

"A week or so," she replied. "I know I should be supportive right now, but I have been trying, and I feel so empty inside. You say you understand what I'm feeling, but you really don't. I'm feeling the same way I did when I left for school, but it's not for a short time; it stays with me all the time. Your body is here, but your mind is far away. I just need some time for myself, that's all."

"Are you thinking of divorcing me?" He had a tone of apprehension in his voice.

Toni's heart jumped when she heard his question. That had never even entered her mind. "Never," she said as a chill swept through her. "I wouldn't even consider divorce as an option. We love each other. We're adults and capable of solving any problem that comes our way."

Michael calmed down after her words. To think that Toni would leave him now when he needed her so badly—it was too much to fathom.

They drove home in silence. Those damn bucket seats! Toni wanted to sit close to him, to hold his hand and allay his fears and nestle her head on his shoulder.

When they reached home, they both changed into their sleepwear and got into bed. They lay together, and Michael caressed her hair, kissing her over and over again. Each kiss was full of a deep tenderness he was seldom able to communicate verbally to her of late. Toni hated putting her sexuality on hold but felt she had no choice and would go crazy if she didn't.

"I love you, honey. Please believe me," Michael whispered.

"I know you do. I never doubted you for a moment."

He reached over and pulled her to him, encircling his arms around her.

"Hold me forever!" she pleaded with him. "Never let me go."

"I never will, honey," he whispered as his lips found hers for the hundredth time.

As the moonlight streamed in through the window, they fell asleep entwined in each other's arms.

The following week, Michael and Toni went to see Leslie. She greeted them warmly as they walked into the office. "Hello, you two," she said with a smile.

"Hello," they responded and sat down.

"How are things going?"

Michael looked at Toni indicating she should speak.

"We're doing our best to get by." Michael nodded in agreement.

"This has been very hard on you both," Leslie said in an understanding tone. "But luckily, Michael is very honest, Toni, and that helps things move along quickly."

"Toni's going to New York the end of this week," Michael interjected.

"Oh, really?"

"My boss is sending me. As I told Michael, I need to get away for a while."

"How do you feel about that, Michael?"

He hesitated for a moment and then said, "Scared."

Toni was surprised at her husband's honesty. So was Leslie. "Why is that?"

"The last time she got on a plane, I never saw her again."

"Well, that's a bit of an exaggeration, isn't it? She's here now."

"You're right. I'm exaggerating, but that's the way I feel."

Leslie turned to Toni. "How do you feel about what he's saying?"

"I know I hurt him when I left, but I was hurting too." She paused for a moment, not wishing to recall that horrible day. "I cried all the way to New York."

Michael gave a start. Toni had never told him that.

"But," she continued, "I wanted him to go with me. He didn't have to go to school. He could have worked while I was in school, just so we wouldn't be separated, but he refused. He became very angry when I asked him."

Silence filled the room. At that point, Leslie didn't want to respond to Toni's words. She sensed that Michael's refusal to go with Toni had something to do with his problems and would wait to discuss that with him alone.

Toni went on. "When I told Michael about my trip to New York, he asked me if I wanted a divorce. I was really shocked. I couldn't believe he had such little faith in me and that I'd be willing to throw in the towel so easily. 'For better or worse'—that's the vow we took. Maybe a lot of people take that lightly, but I don't. I've been very happy with Michael up to now—" Her voice trailed off.

Michael nodded and said, "You will be again, Toni. Please believe me." His eyes were starting to water.

She wanted to go to him and console him, but she didn't.

Leslie interrupted the moment of discomfort by saying, "You came to talk about your sexual problems, isn't that right?"

They both nodded.

"Michael, how are things going for you now?"

"I feel all alone," he said quietly. "I can only blame myself for that. I alienated Toni by not being able to give her what she needs."

Toni put her head down. She felt very sad and lonely. All she wanted was for things to be back to normal.

At that point, Leslie asked Michael to step outside while she spoke with Toni privately.

"I know what you're going through. It's tough, isn't it?"

"I never thought it would be this hard."

"Funny, that's the same thing Michael said."

"Do you know how much longer it'll be?"

"You can't put a time limit on this sort of thing. It also depends on how much Michael is willing to open up about some of his problems."

"Is there anything I can do to help?" Toni asked.

"Don't hold back with him, as painful and frightening as that may seem. Come toward him. Try to show him some form of affection every day. The more he feels that you love him, the sooner he'll feel comfortable about making love."

"I *have* been holding back. I guess I've been acting like a big baby, just thinking about how I've been feeling and not him."

"That's a normal reaction. This type of thing can affect spouses a great deal, but I feel you have the strength to get through it."

"All along, I felt Michael should make the first move and not me."

"He may not be ready to do that. His confidence is shaken now, but your love can help to rebuild it."

"What about our lack of lovemaking?" she asked.

"Well, what I suggested should help bring that along. He's human too. It's four months now since his problems began. I sense he's terrified of losing you right now. You have to instill in him that you're definitely here to stay."

"Should I cancel my trip to New York, then?" Toni asked.

"No, I don't think so, but make the time before you leave quality time, and call him a lot when you get there."

The couple left Leslie's office, and when they got out to the parking lot, Toni put her arms around her husband and hugged him.

"Hey!" He laughed. "What brought that on?"

"I love you, Michael," she said tenderly. "And," she warned, "whether you like it or not, you're stuck with me."

"That's the kind of 'stuck' I don't mind at all." He smiled and gave her nose a quick peck.

"Let's go home, honey."

CHAPTER 15

*T*oni and Michael arrived at the airport awhile before her flight was scheduled to leave. She checked her baggage, and they went up to the observation deck to watch the planes.

"Why didn't you tell me you cried all the way to New York?"

"I don't know," she said quietly. "Pain is not something I like to dwell on."

"I cried that day, too, Toni. I was right here when your plane took off."

She reached for his hand and held it tightly. "I didn't even know that you came to the airport that day."

"I saw the plane board, then came up here and watched you fly away. I don't think I knew what it meant to be miserable until that day. That's why I can't ever lose you again."

"You'll *never* lose me again, mister." She wasn't accustomed to Michael being so insecure. To see him this way hurt her deeply.

"Anyway, I can hear you complaining when we get the phone bill for all the calls I'm going to make." She laughed lightly and he pulled her to him. "Oh, honey, I guess I'm being silly."

"Yes, very silly," Toni agreed.

A few minutes later, they heard her flight being announced and walked slowly to the gate. Michael held her so tightly she thought he was going to break her.

"Michael," she said hesitantly, "I won't go if you don't want me to."

"Am I acting that insecure?" he asked, embarrassed by his behavior. "You should go."

"I'll call you every day," she promised, "and I'll be back before you know I'm gone."

"I'll know you're gone before the plane leaves."

Toni wished she could do something to allay his fears but knew he had to deal with these feelings on his own.

As she walked away to board the plane, Michael came after her. "Here, baby. I forgot to give this to you." He pressed a note into her hand, kissed her lightly, and left.

When Toni settled in her seat, she opened the letter.

My darling Toni,

I guess you think I'm crazy writing my wife a letter, but I need to express what I'm feeling.

You have managed, for the second time, to capture my heart, soul, and my very being. You are the most important person in my life, and no matter what happens, you always will be. I know you'll come back to me. I guess my neurotic side has been out for the past few days.

Please return safely to me.

I love you with all my heart.

Michael

Toni was so touched by the letter, she folded it neatly and held it to her breast. A tear trickled down her cheek as the plane taxied to the runway.

As Michael drove to Leslie's office, he thought of Toni. She would be coming home tomorrow, and he couldn't wait. She was true to her word, calling him every evening at the same time, and sometimes they spent an hour or more on the phone. He couldn't wait for her to return. That particular afternoon, he was feeling terrific, and Leslie immediately noticed it as he walked into her office.

"Well, you're in a good mood today."

He was beaming from one side of his face to the other. "Toni's coming home tomorrow."

"No wonder you're so happy." Leslie laughed.

"I can't wait to see her."

"What will you do when you see her, Michael?" she asked.

"I'm going to grab her, take her home, and make love to her all night!" He blushed at his outburst, and they both laughed.

"I'm happy to hear that. What brought on this change?"

"I had a week away from her and lots of time to think. I've been a real ass, Leslie. Toni is not the cause of my problems. I know that now. I've been blaming her, and she never had anything to do with it."

"Who is then?"

Michael moved nervously in his chair, and his eyes took in the whole room until he was finally able to speak. "My dad." He almost whispered the words, and Leslie had to strain to hear him. Michael looked down at his feet. The silence in the room seemed to last for ages.

Leslie finally said, "Michael?"

He looked up at her, his eyes full of fear.

"Do you want to talk about him?"

"This is really hard," he said heavily.

"I know," she said, "but once you get it out, it won't hurt as much."

"When I was ten, he bought me my first two-wheeler bike. It had no training wheels on it like the other kids' bikes on the block. He told me, 'Get on, son, and ride.' I wanted to do well, I really did, but each time I tried, I would ride for a few seconds and lose my balance. You know what he said to me?" Michael's face was full of hurt. "He said, 'You're a real disappointment to me, son.' He never even bothered showing me how to ride the damn thing."

Leslie's eyes were filled with concern. She shuddered to think what she would hear next. "What happened then, Michael?"

"I threw the bike down and ran into the house. I heard him screaming, 'Get back here, Michael,' but I wouldn't go back. I ran to my room and locked myself in."

Michael put his head in his hands and sobbed violently. "That bastard!" All he ever cared about was himself."

Leslie's heart went out to him. Michael had probably been abused most of his life. God only knows what nightmares she was going to hear. "What did your mother do?"

"I heard him screaming. I think it lasted for a long time, I don't know. Then I heard the door slam and a car drive away. A few minutes later, my mom knocked on my door. She asked to come in. I screamed 'no,' but when she said my father was gone, I got up from the bed and let her in. She had been crying, and her eyes were all swollen. She came to me and put her arms around me. She said, 'He didn't mean it, honey. He just doesn't think. He opens his mouth and hurts people and doesn't realize the damage he does.' I told her I hated him, and she started to cry again. She told me not to ever say that again about my father, then left, and I cried myself to sleep."

Leslie was quiet for a while. Then the silence was broken with Michael's sarcastic laughter.

"Well, that was the start of our beautiful friendship." Fury filled his face.

"Do you want to go on?"

"Why not? The fun's just beginning," he said sourly. "Well, that was when I was ten. Things were pretty quiet most of the time. If he spoke abusively to me, I would block it out. Most of the time, I just avoided him until report card time came along. That was great fun!" Hatred filled his voice. "If I didn't get straight As, he'd throw a fit. He'd tell me how lazy and stupid I was, and no son of his was going to get less than straight As on his report card. My mom would try to intervene, but when he was like that, no one could control him. He'd go into these rages, and his face would turn beet red. I always ran to my room and locked myself in. He'd scream, 'You get down here right now!' and then they'd start to argue. She'd plead with him to leave me alone. It always ended the same way: the door would slam, and my mom would beg my forgiveness. Once I was old enough to have a stereo, it wasn't so bad. I'd run upstairs and blast the music to blot out their fights."

Leslie said at that point it was time to stop, and Michael was relieved to hear it. He decided he'd buy a six-pack on the way home but changed his mind when he realized Toni would be calling.

The following evening, Michael arrived at the airport a short time before Toni's plane was due. He couldn't sit too long and found himself getting up and walking around. His anxiety level was rising as the minutes ticked away. He tried to calm himself, but nothing would work—only seeing Toni.

The plane finally landed, and Michael spotted her immediately. She quickly walked toward him, hesitated for a moment, and then dropped her bags and threw her arms around him, resting her head on his shoulder.

"Hey, I'm supposed to do that."

"Chauvinist," she said playfully.

Michael stood looking at her, feasting on her beauty. "You have no idea how much I missed you."

"Oh, yes I do." She smiled sweetly as he bent down to kiss her. It wasn't just a peck on the cheek, but a deep, tender kiss filled with emotion toward her.

Toni pulled away, embarrassed by his behavior. "Michael, this is a public place. There's people everywhere."

"Oh, no." His eyes filled with love for her. "There's only you and me."

As they drove home, Toni told Michael about her week in New York. She said that the trade show was really good, and she came back with lots of suggestions for her boss. Her leisure time was spent browsing through Chinatown, checking out the wares the street vendors had to offer. She bought some really nice costume jewelry at a fraction of the price and after that had lunch in one of the many wonderful restaurants there. On another day, she went back to F.I.T. to visit her instructors. They were all very happy to see her and pleased at her success. She rambled on about the other places she visited while there, and soon Michael was pulling into the driveway of their apartment building.

Michael brought in Toni's bags, and she said she wanted to take a quick shower.

Michael startled her by asking, "Mind if I join you?"

"Are you sure?"

"Absolutely," he responded, a smile spreading over his face. He came to Toni and pulled her over to the couch. "I've been very wrong about a lot of things." Pain filled his eyes as he recalled how much he must have hurt her. "I blamed you for my problems, and you had nothing to do with them."

"Who did, then?"

"My dad. I just want to make up for all the harm I've done."

Toni's eyes glistened with happiness. "Does that mean that we are going to ..." She never finished the sentence.

Michael pulled her to him and covered her face with wonderfully tender kisses. He murmured in between, "Forgive me, my darling. Please forgive me."

"Oh, Michael—" Her voice overflowed with tenderness.

He lifted her and carried her into the bedroom. Her arms reached to pull him down beside her. As they kissed, she stroked his soft, thick hair and finally implored him, "Make love to me, please." Weeks had passed since they had been together. She felt that the last few moments of waiting were the most unbearable.

He gently kissed her lips as he started to remove her dress.

He removed her bra, and his mouth found its way to her beautiful breasts. She moaned with delight as his mouth moved over them, skillfully employing this tongue until her nipples grew hard under him.

As he kissed her, his hands gently moved down to her panties, stroking her tummy as he went. When he removed them, he found her womanliness blazing like wildfire and bubbling with anticipation.

Toni found her way to his wondrous rod, which sprang up at her touch. Suddenly she wanted to feel it in her mouth, to lick and suck it and please him in a way she never had before.

"I want to kiss you," she whispered as her hand gently stroked his bulk.

He was delighted to hear that, and a moment later, Michael lay nude on the bed before her. She bent over and took his manhood in her soft, sweet mouth. It was so large and as hard as a rock.

"Oh, God," he moaned loudly as her mouth covered it. It felt to him as if his bulk was being enveloped in a delicious hot sea of warmth. Animal sounds came from his wife's mouth as she slowly moved up and down on his manhood. Moments later, he exploded in her, warming the innermost parts of her mouth. She devoured every drop and then smiled up at her husband.

"I love you. I love you," she whispered as he pulled her to him.

He slowly kissed her lips, face, and ears and whispered to her, "Oh, God, that felt so good."

Within seconds, Michael's manhood stood up again like a wooden piling, and they were lost in the rapture of their lovemaking. Slowly and deliberately he moved in and out of her, marveling at every feeling, each emotion communicated by her. As he thrust deeper into her, moving his thick rod in every possible direction, the fire in her core spread wildly until there was no containing it. She grabbed at his back, screaming with rapture as her body burst into climax. Moments later, he joined her in that ecstasy.

They lay there quietly in the wondrous afterglow of their lovemaking. Words were not necessary. Their feelings for each other filled the room with a warmth that was indescribable.

Toni knew their love would last an eternity.

"Will you marry me?"

She laughed quietly, astounded by his question. "We are married."

"But there has to be something after marriage," Michael said. "We can't continue to grow closer as time goes by, can we?"

She answered him by kissing him softly. They fell asleep deep in the glow of their love.

CHAPTER 16

Michael walked into Leslie's office determined he was going to talk about his father. No matter how hard it was, he was going to do it.

"Hello, Michael," Leslie said warmly as he entered.

"Hi. How are things?"

"I'm supposed to ask you that." They both laughed.

"Things couldn't be better. Toni's home, and our lives are back to normal. I feel fantastic."

"I'm so glad to hear that."

"Me too." A grin covered his face.

Leslie was beginning to realize just how charming this young man was.

"Well, shoot away," he said enthusiastically.

"Do you want to talk about your father today?"

"Yes, I do," he said adamantly. "I just want to get 100 percent better. If talking about my dad is going to do it, then that's what I want."

Leslie began to question him. "Now, what age were we at?"

"Well, we were talking about my grades. I guess I was still in elementary school."

"You mean he only hassled you about your grades in elementary school?"

Michael nodded. "When I got into junior high, I became, in his words, 'incorrigible.'"

"He called you that?" Leslie couldn't contain her surprise.

"You wouldn't believe the things he called me."

Oh, yes, I would, she thought to herself.

"Then in junior high school, you made good grades?"

"Average, I'd say."

"Wasn't the pressure harder on you?"

"Not really. I was already becoming my own person and hanging out with my friends most of the time."

"Yes," Leslie said, "but you had to eat, didn't you?"

"My father worked long hours. He was never home before 7:00 p.m., so I'd eat and get out before he came home. Plus, when I was old enough to work, I got a job in a garage close by and worked there three nights a week and on Saturdays. That's how I saved the money for my car."

"So, you spent most of your time avoiding him?"

"Like the plague," Michael said.

"How did your mom feel about that?"

"She never said much. I think she was glad that there was peace in the house. It upset her very much when my father started in on me."

"And then you entered high school?" Leslie asked.

"Yeah," he said, full of nostalgia. "That was a great time for me. I went to the same school as my closest friends and thrived.

I goofed off in my junior year but started getting good grades as a senior—not because of my father but because I wanted to. I excelled in sports and drama. In fact, I was in the class play from tenth grade on."

"Sounds like things were good for you then," Leslie observed.

"They were," he agreed. "I was kind of popular and had some real good friends. Plus, I knew a lot of people in school."

"What else did you do in high school?"

"Well, I was in clubs like Spanish and science."

"And, of course, you met Toni in your senior year, didn't you?"

"Yeah." Michael hesitated a minute, thinking of the past. "I was happy every day with her. It was as if I could speak to her about anything."

"Like your mother, huh?"

"You know, I never thought of it that way. She *is* very much like my mother."

"A boy's mother is usually his first girlfriend, Michael. How he relates to her is how he'll relate to the rest of the women in his life."

"You mean if she's nice, the boy will find a nice girl, and if she's rotten, he'll be attracted to someone bad for him?"

"Yes, that's right," Leslie affirmed.

"Thank God I wasn't a girl!" Michael exclaimed.

Leslie, now as in the past, was always surprised by his perceptiveness. "What caused you to separate?"

"Everything was fine between us. Then I had this big blow-up with my father." Michael's face started to change from a calm expression to one of anxiety. The silence filled the room as if they were in an empty church.

"He started in on me about college. It was one of the few nights he got home early. I told him I wasn't planning on going, and then he exploded. When he got angry, his face looked distorted, like he was wearing an ugly mask or something. I told him my grade-point average wasn't strong enough for me to be admitted to college. My junior year really brought me down. Also, I was seeing Toni a lot and had other activities. I just couldn't improve my average." Michael continued, "He was ranting and raving about what a horrible son I was and such a disappointment to my parents. He said I couldn't do anything right. I blew up at him then. On one hand, I felt good about it, but on the other, I felt I was just as bad as he was."

As Michael recalled the incident, the muscles in his face grew taut, and his tone escalated from anxiety to pure fury. "I screamed back that he was a horrible disappointment as a father and that he never accepted me for who I was. I said all he wanted was for me to be what he wanted—like a robot—and I couldn't be myself around him. I said plenty of things to hurt him that night, but I couldn't help it. Years and years of taking his shit was stored up inside me. I ended up telling him I hated his guts." Unknowingly, tears started to trickle down Michael's face as he spoke.

"He had the nerve to tell me that he loved me. I told him he had a great way of showing it. He told me he only wanted what was best for me, and I said he didn't give a damn about me, just his selfish plans for my life. I don't think I've ever seen my father so broken. As usual, he left the house, but this time he didn't slam the door. He got up quietly, took his coat, and went out. My mother followed, imploring him to come back, but a few minutes later, I heard the car drive off." Michael's fury had grown excessively, and he raged, "That son of a bitch got exactly what he deserved! I'm only sorry I didn't confront him sooner." Then he crumbled in his chair and was overcome with sadness.

"What did I do, Leslie, to be treated that way? What did I do?" The tears trickled down onto his lips.

Leslie was deeply moved by the question. She wished she could lessen his pain but knew that only time would do that. "You did nothing, Michael. You just had an abusive father."

Michael looked up in astonishment. "All these years I thought I was to blame. I loved him. I wanted him to love me back, but the price I had to pay for that love was too much."

"You reacted the way most children do. It's too hard to admit there's something wrong with our parents. We love them and depend on them for nurturing and support. So, you turned it inward."

Michael didn't respond. He just listened to what she had to say and then continued. "After graduation, I started working in construction. I was still living at home, though. I was there until the following October, and then I moved into my own apartment."

"Did you see your father after you moved out?"

"No. I spoke with him once on the phone after I left. He made a point of calling me to tell me that he figured that Toni would never stay with someone like me."

The shock of Michael's words was starting to hit home. He sat there, blindly staring into space.

"Michael?" Leslie tried to bring him back to the present, but a sensation of numbness was sweeping over his body.

"I spoke to my mom and went to see her when he wasn't around, but I didn't see him again until Terri and I got married. And, of course, in public he was always the charming gentleman. If only people knew."

"I think you have some unfinished business with your father."

"The hell I do!" Michael blurted out. "The bastard got exactly what he deserved. He *never* passed up an opportunity to humiliate me."

CHAPTER 17

*M*ichael walked into Leslie's office, six months after he had first met her. She greeted him as usual and then said, "Well, Michael, remember the first day you saw me?"

He laughed uneasily and responded, "How could I forget?"

Leslie went on. "You asked me how long it would take to get through therapy."

"Yes, I remember that," he replied.

"I told you that depended on you. Well, I've thought a great deal about what you told me and have come to what I feel are some pretty sound conclusions."

"You mean this is it?" Michael asked hopefully.

"Yes it is, Michael."

His face filled with happiness as she began. "Now, where do I start? Well, I guess with Toni and the day she left for school."

"I never understood why I couldn't get myself to go with her," Michael said thoughtfully.

"It's not an easy thing to understand. You have two forces inside you, and they're both pulling at you."

"Two forces?" Michael asked, his curiosity growing by the minute.

"Yes, your self-esteem or your estimation of yourself, and feelings of inadequacy or poor self-esteem that your father has instilled in you."

"Inadequacy?" Michael's tone was full of surprise. "I don't understand. I was very popular in school."

"Yes, you were," Leslie agreed. "You were away from home most of the day. Didn't you have teachers who made you feel accepted and special?"

"Yes, I did. My drama teacher and my history teacher. They used to tell me how bright I was all the time, and, yes, my gym teacher did too."

"Your self-esteem was very high then. Also, you had an active sex life and were accepted and liked by your peers and teachers. You managed to bury your feelings of inadequacy deep inside you, and then you met Toni. Didn't something happen between you two when you first met?"

"Yes, I went out with her when I was still going steady with Terri."

"Yes, I remember," Leslie replied. "These feelings of inadequacy tried to push themselves to the surface. That's why you decided not to tell Terri immediately. You weren't sure if you deserved Toni, but she was the girl of your dreams, and your wish to be with her won."

Michael nodded in amazement. Everything was starting to fit together in his mind. "Why wouldn't I go to New York with her then?" he asked, numb from what he was learning.

"Think back to the day you asked her to marry you. Was

it close to the time you had the fight with your father over college?"

"Yes," he said, astonished by her question. "I think it was a few days after."

"If it had been a few days before, my sense is you probably would have been much more receptive to the idea, but that other part of you had reared its ugly head. All your self-doubts came back, and with them came a belief that what your father said was true. You were a disappointment and would never amount to anything in life."

The words stung Michael deep inside, and tears started cascading down his face. He wiped them away and struggled to control his emotions. "Why did I believe that?"

"Why do children believe whatever their parents tell them? Because they love them and depend on them for nurturing. Dad can do no wrong, and if he can't, then it must be true when he tells you that there's something wrong with you. You turned all your anger for your father against yourself and buried it deep inside you."

It was incredible what Leslie was telling Michael. He sat there silently and let the words sink in. "But I couldn't have believed I was no good as a teenager. I *was* popular in school, and I confronted him during that fight."

"Yes, you did, but remember that not only did you have close, loving friends, but you had Toni, who loved and accepted you for exactly who you were. That's why you confronted your father, but the years of conditioning were stronger. He knew exactly what buttons to push to get to you."

There was a deep silence in the room. A few minutes later,

Leslie continued, "When Toni left that day, my sense is that your unconscious was telling you 'It's true what he says. I'll never measure up, in his eyes or hers.'"

Michael began crying again. Soon he was wracked with emotion and sobbing. After some time, he said, "That's why I went away after Toni left. I thought it was only because of her, but it was him too. She was my only way of freeing myself from him, and I lost her."

Leslie said, "Somehow, Toni got mixed up in this. You felt she had turned against you, but in reality, that was your own fury caused by jealous feelings for her."

"Jealous feelings?" Michael's voice was weak with fear.

"Didn't she leave to go to school? Wasn't she going to get what she wanted out of life? And you weren't. You were stuck in St. Paul, working in construction when you really wanted to be an architect." The silence was building in the room, forcing Leslie to continue. "You had your mother, Michael. From what you tell me, she loves you very much."

"Yes, she does," he acknowledged.

"But she loves your father also. It must have torn her apart to see your father treat you that way."

"She tried to intervene," Michael added.

"What I'm trying to point out to you is that she was torn between her love for her husband and for her son. I think she tried to do her best, and she is also why you managed to develop some self-esteem while growing up. It is miraculous that you did, but you had your mom and plenty of friends who accepted you. Your way of dealing with your father was to avoid him as much as possible. You had the inner will to stay away from what made you feel bad."

"Do you think I still have these feelings of inadequacy?" he asked.

"Yes. They came out after your honeymoon, when you withdrew. Is there anything you didn't mention to me that was spoken about on your honeymoon? School, anything?"

"Come to think of it, Toni spoke to me about entering college to study architecture. I remember feeling uncomfortable when she brought it up."

"I think that's what brought out those feelings again. You started to doubt yourself and then your marriage. How could you make her happy if you were 'a disappointment,' as your father would say?"

"I did feel that way," he recalled sadly.

"Again, your father at work. Michael, there is nothing wrong with you. All the problems you have stem from how your father treated you."

Michael sat there quietly thinking about everything Leslie told him. A wonderful feeling of relief filled him. "What do I do now?" he asked quietly.

"You learn to believe in yourself, just as Toni and your mom have always done."

"How do I go about doing that?" he asked, frightened of the answer.

"You find something to boost your self-confidence; for example, going to college."

"College!" Michael jumped at her suggestion, a feeling of doom filling his soul. "You're telling me I should become an architect?"

"Don't you want that, Michael?"

"Yes, but—" Self-doubt filled his mind. "How can I do it?"

"You and Toni will find a way."

Michael put his head in his hands. He was completely overwhelmed by everything he learned that afternoon. He sat there for some time thinking. School? Fear tugged at his heart.

"Michael," Leslie said, "Toni will be here for you, and if you need to talk to me, you know my number."

He lifted his head, his eyes filled with bewilderment. "I never realized how frightened I was about school."

"That's lack of confidence. My sense is that after you get over the first hurdle, you know, get registered and start classes, those fears will disappear quickly."

"I hope you're right," he said doubtfully.

"There's one other thing, Michael—the hard part." He looked at her as she walked around her desk and leaned on it, facing him. "I think you should confront your father."

"My father?" he whispered, a chill running through him.

"Let him know how you feel about what he's done to you."

His lips quivered, and his eyes grew full of apprehension. "I don't know if I can do that."

"Not now," Leslie said, "but in time, when you're stronger."

After six months of analysis, Michael left the office that day not knowing if he should laugh or cry. His childhood suddenly flashed before his eyes. All the fights with his father came back to torment him as his angry face appeared clearly in Michael's mind.

"One day," he promised.

CHAPTER 18

*W*hen Toni returned from work that day, she found Michael in the kitchen wearing her apron. It was nice to be with a man who didn't let traditional roles dictate who he was.

"Hi, honey." She smiled as she walked in the door.

He looked like the old Michael to her, the man she had fallen in love with so many years ago. "Are you okay?" she asked.

"I'm fine. No, I'm better than fine. I'm just great!" His charming smile flooded his face.

"Michael, what happened?" she asked, curious to know what had brought on this transformation.

"I finished therapy today." He acted like a child who just came to a candy store.

Toni ran to him and put her arms around him, ecstatic at the news. "Is it really over?" she asked, only half-believing what she had just heard.

"I've been given a clean bill of health."

"Well, are you going to tell me?" Her curiosity was growing by the minute.

"Uh-huh," he said, "but not until after dinner. I made lasagna." He beamed with pride over his accomplishment.

"I didn't know you could make that." Michael was just full of surprises this evening. It seemed like every day she was learning new things about him.

Dinner was wonderful. With the lasagna, Michael served soup, salad, cooked vegetables, bread and white wine he had bought especially for the occasion.

After coffee, they sat in the living room, and Michael related everything Leslie had told him during the session.

Toni sat there stunned. What she was hearing was too shocking to believe. Her Michael an abused child? And by the man she had always thought was sweet and kind?

"That's probably why you didn't break up with Terri until I forced you to."

"Why?" Michael asked, too weary to think.

"Because you probably felt you weren't good enough for me."

He agreed with what she was saying. She went on, wishing for answers to clear up the mystery in her mind.

"What about your mom? She loves you very much."

"And him too," Michael added. "She just wanted peace in the family."

"But Michael, at our wedding you told me your dad was very kind to you."

"That was the first kind words he'd said to me in years."

"It's a start, honey."

"What do you mean it's a start?" He asked, anger filling his voice.

"For you and your dad to work out your problems."

"I worked out my problems with him a long time ago," Michael shouted, startled by the suggestion. He walked into the bedroom and stretched out on the bed. "I can't talk about this now," he said, emotionally exhausted by the day's events.

Toni sat down beside him and said softly, "When you're ready to confront him, you will."

"I may never be ready for that," Michael replied weakly.

"We'll see," Toni responded.

CHAPTER 19

The next five years passed quickly for Michael and Toni. Their first year was spent in New York City, where they both worked and Michael attended school in the evening. Because of his low grade-point average, the only way of getting into the U of M was to transfer from another college with a good average.

Toni was sorry to leave St. Paul and her job at Shapiro's, but she hoped she would somehow get the job back when they returned.

Once Michael began at the U of M, most of his time was spent studying. It created a strain on their relationship, but Toni was busy with her own work, and they made time for each other whenever they could.

After a year of working for Shapiro's competitor, Toni was asked to return to her old job as head designer. She was thrilled to no end.

She kept in touch with Michael's mother over the years. Madeline was always pleased to hear of his progress. When his graduation drew near, she called her. This would be a double celebration. Not only did he earn his master's degree, but he also landed a job with one of the most prestigious architectural firms in St. Paul.

"Madeline, how are you?" she asked.

"Hi, honey. How is everything going?"

"Really well. In fact, I'm calling because Michael will be graduating next month and also, he just landed a job at Simsons."

"That's wonderful news." Madeline had a hard time getting the words out, she was so choked with emotion. "I'm so proud of him, Toni."

"Me too."

"I was thinking how nice it would be if we could throw a party for him."

"That's a wonderful idea. Where were you planning on having it?"

"Well, our apartment is kind of small," Toni hinted.

"Oh, I see what you're getting at. Has this anything to do with John?" she suggested.

"A great deal," Toni admitted. "Don't you think it's about time they settled their differences?"

"Your timing is perfect." Madeline said with a laugh.

On Michael's graduation day, he rose early, unable to sleep any longer. Although he tried to be quiet, his excitement got the best of him, and he paced back and forth through the apartment, unable to contain his nervousness.

Toni got out of bed and stood smiling at him. "Well, mister, you did it," she said joyfully.

He beamed with excitement, and she came to him and

hugged him. "Yes, I did." He was very pleased with himself, and Toni knew that his dreams were finally coming true.

"I have a surprise for you, honey," she said mischievously. "Right after graduation, we're going somewhere, but don't ask any questions, and I'll have to blindfold you."

Michael laughed. He wasn't sure what she had planned, but he didn't care. He was walking on air and would go anywhere she wanted.

The graduation ceremony had been impressive. Toni recalled how handsome Michael looked in his cap and gown. Her heart swelled with pride for him, admiring his tremendous courage. He had managed to overcome many of his problems and come out a winner. She wondered if, in the same situation, she could have been as strong as he.

"Michael Jameson."

Toni's heart jumped when she heard his name called out. She knew at this moment that his parents were feeling the same emotions as she. She had arranged to get them tickets to the commencement exercises, and they were out there somewhere.

When it was all over, Toni managed to find Michael in the throng of people. His parents had gone back to their home to greet the guests when they arrived. Many people were invited to Michael's surprise party: relatives from both families, close friends, and classmates from college and high school.

"I think I'll take this off," Michael reached to remove his cap.

"Oh no, you don't," Toni insisted. "The only other time you looked this handsome was our wedding day. I intend to enjoy you for a while."

Michael laughed at Toni, pleased that she was making such

a fuss over his graduation. He wondered where she was taking him. When they got in the car, Toni handed him the blindfold and teased, "No peeking now."

Michael lifted his right hand in jest and exclaimed playfully, "Yes, my lady and mistress!" They giggled simultaneously.

The weather was beautiful in St. Paul that day. As they drove toward the Jamesons' home, Toni thought of how wonderful life was with Michael. She secretly prayed that he would be able to solve his one last problem.

When they pulled into the driveway, Toni came around and guided Michael up the path to the backyard. They could hear music playing and people laughing.

"Hey, what's going on?" he asked.

"You'll see soon." Toni tried to contain her excitement.

A moment later, Toni removed the blindfold, and Michael stood there in amazement as his friends and family yelled out, "Surprise!"

He looked at his father, and John Jameson smiled weakly at his son. Michael's heart went out to him. Over the years, he had made peace with the anger he felt for his father, and now all that remained was a sense of pity for the man. Try as he may, he could never push himself to confront him. He turned to Toni, standing by his side, and kissed her. He was beginning to understand what this was all about.

The party lasted the whole afternoon with people dancing, drinking, and enjoying themselves. Michael had plenty of time to greet and speak with friends he hadn't seen in years. Toni also enjoyed herself, dancing with her father and brother and speaking with Michael's parents and friends.

Around eight o'clock in the evening, people started to depart. As more people left, Michael noticed his father sitting alone. He vowed *never* to treat his son the way this man had treated him. Michael walked over to where he was sitting and looked down at him. For a few moments, John Jameson wasn't aware someone was standing over him, appearing to be deep in thought. He looked up and saw Michael, and a look of surprise crossed his face.

"Hello, son," he said meekly and motioned for him to sit next to him. "It's been a long time, Michael."

"I know," Michael responded quietly, his heart beating with apprehension.

"I missed you very much. Your mother told me you always called, but you never asked to speak with me."

"I was too angry with you," he muttered.

"Michael ..." His father's voice trailed off.

"Why did you treat me like that?" Michael's voice was broken with emotion. "All those years of abuse! And what did I ever do to you?"

"Would you believe me if I told you?" a lonely, tired man answered his son.

"Tell me," Michael urged him.

"I hated my father. He treated me like a dog when I was a boy, and then I grew up to treat you the same way."

"But you had a choice. You didn't have to do that."

"I didn't know at the time that I did. Oh, your mom would always try to talk some sense into me, but nothing helped until you moved out and I realized that I had lost you. It took me a long time to realize all the wrong I did. I turned all my anger for my father against you. Your mother, God bless her, made me aware of it."

Michael sat there silently, not knowing what to say. Finally, his father broke the silence. "I've treated you very badly, Michael. Everything you said when we had that fight was true. I was the disappointment—not you!" John Jameson forced himself to hold back his tears.

"Will you forgive me, son?" his father asked with a pleading look in his eyes.

Michael saw before him a sad, broken man who had suffered greatly by the absence of his son. His heart was full of pity for his father.

As he stood up, he felt as if a burden of many years had been lifted from him. He had finally found himself. The odds were against that happening, but he defied them and won.

He knew then that he could continue punishing his father by staying away or he could forgive him, and they could both start to live again.

"Dad," he said.

His father looked up with surprise.

"Would you like to come to dinner next week?"

John stood up, and this time he couldn't hold back the tears. Michael put his arms around him and drew him close. He wasn't aware that he was crying too.

"I feel like a baby crying like this," his father apologized for his behavior.

"But does it make you feel better?"

"You know what? It really does."

Madeline and Toni watched their guys from the kitchen

window. They smiled and hugged each other. After many years, peace had finally come to the Jameson family.

Some time later, Toni found a letter in her mailbox from Central High School. She opened and read

10th Annual Reunion
sponsored by
the
Alumni Association
for
the
Class of 1967

When she told Michael about it, he expressed a wish to go, wondering how their old high school friends' lives had turned out.

That evening, as Toni and Michael entered their alma mater, Michael commented, "It all started here, honey."

"I know." She smiled sweetly and squeezed his hand.

The evening was a real eye-opener for the couple. They saw Sheryl, who was working as a secretary and was divorced with two children. Michael saw friends he hadn't seen in years who were in a variety of fields, from telephone linemen to lawyers. He realized that night, economic security was not the key to success but how one feels about oneself.

As the party drew to a close, Michael and Toni said their good-byes and headed for the door.

"Honey," Michael said, once they were outside, "don't you think it's about time we thought about starting a family?"

Pleased by the question, Toni responded, "I don't know. Are you good at changing diapers?" They both giggled and headed for the Mustang. When they got to the car, Michael stood and searched for his keys. Toni asked, "Does that mean no more bucket seats, Mr. Jameson?"

He smiled tenderly at his loving wife and blew her a kiss from his side of the car.

T, T RICIA B ARISONZI-J OHNSON, was born in St. Paul, Minnesota. At the age of nineteen, she left to pursue a career in fashion design in New York City. She holds an associate's degree in applied sciences from the Fashion Institute of Technology and a bachelor of arts in Spanish from Hunter College. Her passions include writing poetry, photography, and translating English songs into Spanish and singing them. She currently resides in New York City.

CPSIA information can be obtained
at www.ICGtesting.com
Printed in the USA
BVHW07*0940230718
522386BV00008B/62/P